Also by John Updike

BECH IS BACK

John Updike

BECH

IS BACK

Alfred A. Knopf   New York

1982

THIS IS A BORZOI BOOK
PUBLISHED BY ALFRED A. KNOPF, INC.

"Australia and Canada," "Bech Third-Worlds It," and
"The Holy Land" originally appeared in Playboy magazine.
"Three Illuminations in the Life of an American Author"
originally appeared in The New Yorker.

Library of Congress Cataloging in Publication Data
Updike, John.
Bech is back.
Contents: Three illuminations in the life of an
American author—Bech third-worlds it—Australia
and Canada—The Holy Land—[etc.]
I. Title. PS3571.P4B44 813'.54 82-161
ISBN 0-394-52806-9 AACR2
ISBN 0-394-52849-2 Limited edition

Manufactured in the United States of America
FIRST EDITION

BECQUE (Henry) . . . *Après des débuts poé-*
tiques assez obscurs . . . à travers des inexpériences
et des brutalités voulues, un talent original et
vigoureux. Toutefois, l'auteur ne reparut que
beaucoup plus tard avec [œuvres nombreuses],
où la critique signals les mêmes défauts et la même
puissance. . . . M. Becque a été décoré de la
Légion d'honneur en 1887.

—LA GRANDE ENCYCLOPÉDIE

Contents

BECH IS BACK

Three Illuminations in the Life
of an American Author

THOUGH HENRY BECH, the author, in his middle years had all but ceased to write, his books continued, as if ironically, to live, to cast shuddering shadows toward the center of his life, where that thing called his reputation cowered. To have once imagined and composed fiction, it seemed, laid him under an indelible curse of unreality. The phone rang in the middle of the night and it was a kid on a beer trip wanting to argue about the ambivalent attitude toward Jewishness expressed (his professor felt) in *Brother Pig*. "Embrace your ethnicity, man," Bech was advised. He hung up, tried to estimate the hour from the yellowness of the Manhattan night sky, and as the yellow turned to dawn's pearl gray succumbed to the petulant embrace of interrupted sleep. Next morning, he looked to himself, in the bathroom mirror, markedly reduced. His once leonine head, and the frizzing hair expressive of cerebral energy, and the jowls testimonial to companionable bourbon taken in midnight discourse with Philip

Rahv were all being whittled by time, its relentless wizen-ing. The phone rang and it was a distant dean, suddenly a buddy, inviting him to become a commencement speaker in Kansas. "Let me be brutally frank," the dean said in his square-shouldered voice. "The seniors' com-mittee voted you in unanimously, once Ken Kesey turned us down. Well, there was one girl who had to be talked around. But it turned out she had never read your stuff, just Kate Millett's condemnation of the rape bits in *Travel Light*. We gave her an old copy of *When the Saints*, and now she's your staunchest fan. Not to put any unfair pressure on, but you don't want to break that girl's heart. Or do you?"

"I do," Bech solemnly affirmed. But since the dean denied him the passing grade of a laugh, the author had to babble on, digging himself deeper into the bottomless apology his unproductive life had become. He heard himself, unreally, consenting. The date was months away, and World War III might intervene. He hung up, reflecting upon the wonderful time warps of the literary life. You stay young and merely promising for-ever. Five years of silence, even ten, pass as a pause un-noticed by the sluggish, reptilian race of critics. An eighteen-year-old reads a book nearly as old as he is and in his innocent mind you are born afresh, your pen just lifted from the page. Bech could rattle around forever amid the persisting echoes, being "himself," going to parties and openings in his Henry Bech mask. He had his friends, his fans, even his collectors. Indeed, his phone over the lengthening years acknowledged no more faith-ful agitator than that foremost collector of Bechiana,

Marvin Federbusch, of Cedar Meadow, Pennsylvania.
The calls had begun to come through shortly after the
publication of his first novel in 1955. Would Mr. Bech be
so kind as to consider signing a first edition if it were
mailed with a stamped, self-addressed padded envelope?
Of course, the young author agreed, flattered by the suggestion that there had been a second edition and somewhat amused by the other man's voice, which was
peculiarly rich and slow, avuncular and patient, with a
consonant-careful accent Bech associated with his own
German-Jewish forebears. Germanic thoroughness char-
acterized, too, the bibliographical rigor as, through the
years, the invisible Federbusch kept up with Bech's once
burgeoning production and even acquired such ephemera
as Bech's high-school yearbook and those wartime copies
of *Collier's* and *Liberty* in which his first short stories
had appeared. As Bech's creativity—checked by the rude
critical reception given his massive chef-d'oeuvre, *The
Chosen*,* and then utterly stymied within the mazy ambitions of his work in progress, tentatively titled *Think*

---

* Not to be confused with *The Chosen*, by Chaim Potok (New
York: Simon & Schuster, 1967). Nor with *The Chosen*, by Ed-
ward J. Edwards (London: P. Davies, 1950); *The Chosen*, by
Harold Uriel Ribalow (London: Abelard-Schuman, 1959); *Chosen
Country*, by John Dos Passos (Boston: Houghton Mifflin, 1951);
A Chosen Few, by Frank R. Stockton (New York: Charles
Scribner's Sons, 1895); *The Chosen Four*, by John Theodore
Tussaud (London: Jonathan Cape, 1928); *The Chosen Highway*,
by Lady Blomfield (London: The Bahá'i Publishing Trust, 1940);
Chôsen-koseki-kenkyû-kwai (Seoul: Keijo, 1934); *The Chosen
One*, by Rhys Davies (London: Heinemann, 1967); *The Chosen
One*, by Harry Simonhoff (New York: T. Yoseloff, 1964); *The
Chosen People*, by Sidney Lauer Nyburg (Philadelphia: J. B. Lip-
pincott, 1917); *The Chosen Place, the Timeless People*, by Paule
Marshall (New York: Harcourt, Brace & World, 1969); *The
Chosen Valley*, by Margaret Irene Snyder (New York: W. W.

Big—ceased to supply objects for collection, a little flurry of reprinting occurred, and unexpected foreign languages (Korean, Turkish) shyly nudged forward and engorged some one of those early works which Bech's celebrated impotence had slowly elevated to the status of minor classics. Federbusch kept a retinue of dealers busy tracking down these oddments, and the books all came in time to the author's drafty, underpopulated apartment at Ninety-ninth and Riverside for him to sign and send back. Bech learned a lot about himself this way. He learned that in Serbo-Croatian he was bound with Washington Irving as a Hudson Valley regionalist, and that in Paraguay *The Chosen* was the choice of a book club whose honorary chairman was General Alfredo Stroessner. He learned that the Japanese had managed to issue more books by him than he had written, and that the Hungarians had published on beige paper a bulky symposium upon Kerouac, Bech, and Isaac Asimov. On his Brazilian jackets Bech looked swarthy, on his Finnish pale and icy-eyed, and on his Australian a bit like a kangaroo. All these varied volumes arrived from Federbusch and returned to Federbusch; the collector's voice gradually deepened over the years to a granular, all-forgiving grandfatherliness. Though Bech as man and artist had turned skimpy and scattered, Federbusch was out there in the blue beyond the Hudson gathering up what pieces there were. What Federbusch didn't collect deserved oblivion—deserved to fall, the dross of Bech's

Norton, 1948); *Chosen Vessels*, by Parthene B. Chamberlain (New York: T. Y. Crowell & Co., 1882); *Chosen Words*, by Ivor Brown (London: Jonathan Cape, 1955); or *Choses d'autrefois*, by Ernest Gagnon (Quebec: Dussault & Proulx, 1905).

days, into the West Side gutters and be whipped into somebody's eye by the spring winds.

The author in these thin times supported himself by appearing at colleges. There, he was hauled from the creative-writing class to the faculty cocktail party to the John D. Benefactor Memorial Auditorium and thence, baffled applause still ringing in his ears, back to the Holiday Inn. Once, in central Pennsylvania, where the gloomy little hilltop schools are stocked with starch-fed students blinking like pupfish after their recent emergence from fundamentalism, Bech found himself with an idle afternoon, a rented car, and a map that said he was not far from Cedar Meadow. The fancy took him to visit Federbusch. He became, in his mind's eye, a god descending—whimsical as Zeus, radiant as Apollo. The region needed radiance. The heavy ghost of coal hung everywhere. Cedar Meadow must have been named in a fit of rural nostalgia, for the town was a close-built brick huddle centered on a black river and a few gaunt factories slapped up to supply Grant's murderous armies. The unexpected reality of this place, so elaborate and layered in its way, so El Grecoesque and sad between its timbered hills, beneath its grimy clouds, so remote in its raw totality from the flattering bookishness that had been up to now its sole purchase on Bech's mind, nearly led him to drive through it, up its mean steep streets and down, and on to tomorrow's Holiday Inn, near a Mennonite normal school.

But he passed a street whose name, Belleview, had been rendered resonant by over fifteen years of return book envelopes: Marvin Federbusch, 117 Belleview. The haggard street climbed toward its nominal view past retaining walls topped with stone spikes; on the slanted street corners there were grocery stores of a type Bech remembered from the Thirties, in the upper Bronx, the entrances cut on the diagonal, the windows full of faded cardboard inducements. He found number 117: corroded aluminum numerals marked a flight of cement steps divided down the middle by an iron railing. Bech parked, and climbed. He came to a narrow house of bricks painted red, a half-house actually, the building being divided down the middle like the steps, and the tones of red paint not quite matching. The view from the gingerbread porch was of similar houses, as close-packed as dominoes arrayed to topple, and of industrial smokestacks rising from the river valley, and of bluish hills gouged by abandoned quarrying. The doorbell distantly stridulated. A small shapeless woman in her sixties answered Bech's ring. "My brother's having his rest," she said.

Her black dress had buttons all down the front; her features seemed to be slightly rolling around in her face, like the little brass beads one maddeningly tries as a child to settle in their cardboard holes, in those dexterity-teasing toys that used to come with Cracker Jack.

"Could you tell him Henry Bech is here?"

Without another word, and without admitting him to the house, she turned away. Federbusch was so slow to arrive, Bech supposed that his name had not been conveyed correctly, or that the collector could not believe that the object of fifteen years of devotion had miraculously appeared in person.

But Federbusch, when he came at last, knew quite

: 8 :

well who Bech was. "You look older than on your chackets," he said, offering a wan smile and a cold, hard handshake.

This was the voice, but the man looked nothing like it—sallow and sour, yet younger than he should have been, with not an ounce of friendly fat on him, in dark trousers, white shirt, and suspenders. He was red-eyed from his nap, and his hair, barely flecked by gray, stood straight up. The lower half of his face had been tugged into deep creases by the drawstrings of some old concluded sorrow. "It's nice of you to come around," he said, as if Bech had just stepped around the corner—as if Cedar Meadow were not the bleak far rim of the world but approximately its center. "Come on in, why don'tcha now?"

Within, the house held an airless slice of the past. The furniture looked nailed-down and smelled pickled. Nothing had been thrown away; invisible hands, presumably those of the sister, kept everything in order—the glossy knickknacks and the doilies and the wedding photos of their dead parents and the landscapes a dead aunt had painted by number and the little crystal dishes of presumably petrified mints. Oppressive ranks of magazines—*Christian Age*, *Publishers Weekly*, the journal of the Snyder County Historical Society—lay immaculate on a lace-covered table, beneath an overdressed window whose sill was thick with plastic daffodils. In the corners of the room, exposed plumbing pipes had been papered in the same paper as the walls. The ceilings, though high, had been papered, too. Kafka was right, Bech saw: life is a matter of burrows. Federbusch beside him was giving off a strange withered scent—the delicate stink of affront. Bech guessed he had been too frankly looking around, and said, to cover himself, "I don't see my books."

Even this missed the right note. His host intoned, in the sonorous voice Bech was coming to hear as funereal, "They're kept in a closet, so the sun won't fade the chackets."

A room beyond this stagnant front parlor had a wall of closet doors. Federbusch opened one, hastily closed it, and opened another. Here indeed was a trove of Bechiana —old Bech in *démodé* Fifties jackets, reprinted Bech in jazzy Seventies paperbacks with the silver lettering of witchcraft novels, Bech in French and German, Danish and Portuguese, Bech anthologized, analyzed, and de-luxized, Bech laid to rest. The books were not erect in rows but stacked on their sides like lumber, like dubious ingots, in this lightless closet along with—oh, treachery! —similarly exhaustive, tightly packed, and beautifully unread collections of Roth, Mailer, Barth, Capote. . . . The closet door was shut before Bech could catalogue every one of the bedfellows the promiscuous Federbusch had captivated.

"I don't have any children myself," the man was saying mournfully, "but for my brother's boys it'll make a wonderful inheritance some day."

"I can hardly wait," Bech said. But his thoughts were sad. His thoughts dwelt upon our insufficient tragedies, our dreadfully musty private lives. How wrong he had been to poke into this burrow, how right Federbusch was to smell hurt! The greedy author, not content with adoration in two dimensions, had offered himself in a fatal third, and maimed his recording angel. "My dealer just sent some new Penguins," Federbusch said, mumbling in shame, "and it would save postage if . . ." Bech signed the paperbacks and wound his way through ravaged hills to the Mennonite normal school, where he mocked the students' naïve faith and humiliated himself with drunkenness at the reception afterward at the Holiday Inn. But no atonement could erase his affront to Federbusch, who never troubled his telephone again.

In the days when Bech was still attempting to complete *Think Big*, there came to him a female character who might redeem the project, restore its lost momentum and focus. She was at first the meagerest wisp of a vision, a "moon face" shining with a certain lightly perspiring brightness over the lost horizon of his plot. The pallor of this face was a Gentile pallor, bearing the kiss of Nordic fogs and frosts, which ill consorted with the urban, and perforce Jewish, hurly-burly he was trying to organize. Great novels begin with tiny hints—the sliver of madeleine melting in Proust's mouth, the shade of louse-gray that Flaubert had in mind for Mme. Bovary—and Bech had begun his messy accumulation of pages with little more than a hum, a hum that kept dying away, a hum perhaps spiritual twin to the rumble of the IRT under Broadway as it was felt two blocks to the west, on the sixth floor, by a bored bachelor. The hum, the background radiation to the universe he was trying to create, was, if not the meaning of life, the tenor of meaninglessness in our late-twentieth-century, post-numinous, industrial-consumeristic civilization, North American branch, Middle Atlantic subdivision. Now this hum was pierced by an eerie piping from this vague "moon face."

Well, the woman would have to be attractive; women in fiction always are. From the roundness of her face, its innocent pressing frontality, would flow a certain "bossiness," a slightly impervious crispness that would set her at odds with the more subtle, ironical, conflicted, slippery intelligentsia who had already established power positions in the corporate structure of his virtually bankrupt fantasy. Since this moony young (for the crispness, this lettucy taste of hers, bespoke either youth or intense refrigeration) woman stood outside the strong family and business ties already established, she would have to be a mistress. But whose? Bech thought of assigning her to Tad Greenbaum, the six-foot-four, copiously freckled, deceptively boyish dynamo who had parlayed a gagwriter's servitude into a daytime-television empire. But Tad already had a mistress—stormy, raven-haired, profoundly neurotic Thelma Stern. Also, by some delicate gleam of aversion, the moon face refused to adhere to Greenbaum. Bech offered her instead to Thelma's brother Dolf, the crooked lawyer, with his silken mustaches, his betraying stammer, and his great clean glass desk. Bech even put the two of them into bed together; he loved describing mussed sheets, and the sea-fern look of trees seen from the window of a sixth-floor apartment, and the way the chimney pots of the adjacent roofs resemble tin men in black pajamas engaged in slow-motion burglary. But though the metaphors prospered, the relationship didn't take. No man was good enough for this woman, unless it were Bech himself. She must have a name. Moon face, Morna—no, he already had a Thelma, his new lady was cooler, aloof . . . doom, Poe, Lenore. *And the only word there spoken was the whispered word, "Lenore!"* Lenore would do. Her work? That kindly bossiness, that confident frontality—the best he could think of was to make her an assistant producer for his imaginary network. But that wasn't right: it didn't account for her supernatural serenity.

She became as real to him as the nightglow on his ceiling during insomnia. He wrote scenes of her dressing and undressing, in the space between the mussed bed-sheets and the window overlooking treetops and chimney pots; he conjured up a scene where Lenore primly lost her temper and told Tad Greenbaum he was a tyrant. Tad fired her, then sent Thelma around to persuade her not to write an exposé for *TV Tidbits*. Experimenting with that curious androgynous cool Lenore possessed, Bech put her into bed with Thelma, to see what happened. Plenty happened, perhaps more gratifyingly to the author than to either character; if he as male *voyeur* had not been present, they might have exchanged verbal parries and left each other's yielding flesh untouched. However, Thelma, Bech had previously arranged, had become pregnant by her ex-husband, Polonius Stern, and could not be allowed a Sapphic passion that would pull Lenore down into the plot. He cancelled the pregnancy but the moon face hung above the plot still detached, yet infusing its tangle with a glow, a calm, a hope that this misbegotten world of Bech's might gather momentum. She seemed, Lenore, to be drawing closer.

One night, reading at the New School, he became conscious of her in the corner of his eye. Over by the far wall, at the edge of the ocean of reading-attending faces —the terrible tide of the up-and-coming, in their thuggish denims and bristling beards, all their boyhood misdemeanors and girlhood grievances still to unpack into print, and the editors thirsty to drink their fresh blood, their contemporary slant—Bech noticed a round female face, luminous, raptly silent. He tried to focus on her, lost his place in the manuscript, and read the same sentence twice. It echoed in his ears, and the audience tittered; they were embarrassed for him, this old dead whale embalmed in the anthologies and still trying to spout. He kept his eyes on his pages, and when he lifted his gaze, at last, to relieved applause, Lenore had vanished, or else he had lost the place in the hall where she had been seated. *Quaff, oh quaff this kind nepenthe and forget this lost Lenore!*

A week later, at his reading at the YMHA, she had moved closer, into the third or fourth row. Her wide, white, lightly perspiring face pressed upward in its intensity of attention, refusing to laugh even when those all around her did. As Bech on the high stage unrolled, in his amplified voice, some old scroll of foolery, he outdid himself with comic intonations to make his milk-pale admirer smile; instead, she solemnly lowered her gaze now and then to her lap, and made a note. Afterward, in the unscheduled moment of siege that follows a reading, she came backstage and waited her turn in the pushing crowd of autograph-seekers. When at last he dared turn to her, she had her notebook out. Was this truly

Lenore? Though he had failed to imagine some details (the little gold hoop earrings, and the tidy yet full-bodied and somewhat sensually casual way in which she had bundled her hair at the back of her head), her physical presence flooded the translucent, changeable skin of his invention with a numbing concreteness. He grabbed reflexively at her notebook, thinking she wanted him to sign it, but she held on firmly, and said to him, "I thought you'd like to know. I noted three words you mispronounced. 'Hectare' is accented on the first syllable and the 'e' isn't sounded. In 'flaccid' the first 'c' is hard. And 'sponge' is like 'monkey'—the 'o' has the quality of a short 'u.' "

"Who are you?" Bech asked her.

"A devotee." She smiled, emphasizing the long double "e." Another devotee pulled Bech's elbow on his other side, and when he turned back, Lenore was gone. *Darkness there and nothing more.*

He revised what he had written. The scene with Thelma was sacred filth, dream matter, not to be touched; but the professional capacities of the moon face had come clearer—she was a schoolteacher. A teacher of little children, children in the first-to-fourth-grade range, in some way unusual, whether unusually bright or with learning disabilities he couldn't at first decide. But as he wrote, following Lenore into her clothes and the elevator and along the steam-damp, slightly tipping streets of West Side Manhattan, the name above the entrance of the building she entered became legible: she taught in a Steiner School. Her connection with the other characters of *Think Big* must be, therefore, through their children.

Bech rummaged back through the manuscript to discover whether he had given Tad Greenbaum and his long-suffering wife, Ginger, boys or girls for children, and what ages. He should have made a chart. Faulkner and Sinclair Lewis used to. But Bech had always resisted those practical aids which might interfere with the essential literary process of daydreaming; Lenore belonged to a realm of subconscious cumulus. She would have wide hips: the revelation came to him as he slipped a week's worth of wastepaper into a plastic garbage bag. But did the woman who had come up to him, in fact, have wide hips? It had been so quick, so magical, he had been conscious only of her torso in the crowd. He needed to see her again, as research.

When she approached him once more, in the great hot white tent annually erected for the spring ceremonial of the American Academy on those heights beyond Harlem, she was wearing a peasant skirt and braless purple bodice, as if to hasten in the summer. To be dressy she had added a pink straw hat; the uplifted gesture with which she kept the wide hat in place opened up a new dimension in the character of Lenore. She had been raised amid greenery, on, say, a Hardyesque farm in northeastern Connecticut. Though her waist was small, her hips were ample. The sultriness of the tent, the spillage of liquor from flexible plastic cups, the heavy breathing of Bech's fellow immortals made a romantic broth in which her voice was scarcely audible; he had to stoop, to see under her hat and lip-read. Where was her fabled "bossiness" now? She said, "Mr. Bech, I've been working up my nerve to ask, would you ever consider coming and talking to my students? They're so sweet and confused, I try to expose them to people with values, any values. I had a porno film director, a friend of a friend, in the other day, so it's nothing to get uptight about. Just be yourself." Her eyes were dyed indigo by the shadow of the hat, and her lips, questing, had a curvaceous pucker he had never dreamed of.

Bech noticed, also, a dark-haired young woman standing near Lenore, wearing no makeup and a man's tweed jacket. A friend, or the friend of a friend? The young woman, seeing the conversation about to deepen, drifted away. Bech asked, "How old are your students?"

"Well, they're in the third grade now, but it's a Steiner School—"

"I know."

"—and I move up with them. You might be a little wasted on them now; maybe we should wait a few years, until they're in fifth."

"And I've had time to work on my pronunciation."

"I do apologize if that seemed rude. It's just a shock, to realize that a master of words doesn't hear them in his head the way you do." As she said this, her own pronunciation seemed a bit slurred. An empty plastic glass sat in her hand like an egg collected at dusk.

Perhaps it was the late-afternoon gin, perhaps the exhilaration of having just received a medal (the Melville Medal, awarded every five years to that American author who has maintained the most meaningful silence), but this encounter enchanted Bech. The questing fair face perspiring in the violet shade of the pink hat, the happy clatter around him of writers not writing, the thrusting smell of May penetrating the tent walls, the little electric push of a fresh personality—all felt too good to be true. He felt, deliciously, overpowered, as reality always overpowers fiction.

He asked her, "But will we still be in touch, when your sweet confused students are in the fifth grade?"

"Mr. Bech, that's up to you." In the shade of her hat, she lowered her eyes.

"To me?"

Her blue eyes lifted boldly. "Who else?"

"How do you feel about dinner then, if we can find the flap to get out of this tent?"

"The two of us?"

"Who else?" *Of course*, he was thinking, with the voice of reason that dismally mutters accompaniment to every euphoria, *there is a rational explanation. God forbid there wouldn't be a rational explanation. I have conjured this creature, by eye-glance and inflection, from the blank crowds just as I conjured her, less persuasively, from blank paper.* "What did you say your name was?"

"Ellen," she said.

So he had got that slightly wrong. He had been slightly wrong in a hundred details, the months revealed. Their affair did not last until her students were in the fifth grade. It was his literary side, it turned out, his textbook presence, that she loved. Also, she really did—his instincts had been right in this—see the male sex as, sexually, second-rate. Still, she gave him enough of herself to eclipse, to crush, "the rare and radiant maiden whom the angels name Lenore," and once again *Think Big* ground to a grateful halt.

Three Illuminations

. . .

An irresistible invitation came to Bech. A subsidiary of the Superoil Corporation called Superbooks had launched a series of signed classics; for an edition of *Brother Pig* bound in genuine pigskin Bech was invited to sign twenty-eight thousand five hundred tip-in sheets of high-rag-content paper, at the rate of one dollar fifty a sheet. He was to do this, furthermore, during a delightful two-week holiday on a Caribbean island, where Superoil owned a resort. He should take with him a person to pull the sheets as he signed them. This "puller" could be a friend, or someone hired in the locality. All this was explained to Bech as to a fairly stupid child by a hollow-voiced man calling from corporation headquarters—a thousand-acre variant of Disneyland somewhere in Delaware.

As always in the face of good fortune, Bech tended to cringe. "Do I have to have a puller?" he asked. "I've never had an agent."

"The answer to your question," the man from Superbooks said, "is one-hundred-percent affirmative. From our experience, without a puller efficiency tapers very observably. As I say, we can hire one on the spot and train her."

Bech imagined her, a svelte little Carib who had been flown to emergency secretarial school, but doubted he could satisfy her after the first proud rush. So he asked Norma Latchett to be his puller.

Her reply was inevitable. "Super," she said.

In weary truth, Bech and Norma had passed beyond

the end of their long romance into a limbo of heterosexual palship haunted by silently howling abandoned hopes. They would never marry, never be fruitful. The little island of San Poco was a fit stage for their end drama—the palm trees bedraggled and battered from careless storage in the prop room, the tin-and-tarpaper houses tacked together for a short run, the boards underfoot barely covered by a sandy thin soil resembling coffee grounds, the sea a piece of rippling silk, the sunshine as harsh, white, and constant as overhead spotlights. The island was littered with old inspirations—a shoal collecting the wrecks of hotels, night spots, cabañas, and eateries swamped by the brilliant lethargy. The beach resort where Bech and Norma and the twenty-eight thousand five hundred pieces of paper were housed had been built by pouring cement over inflated balloons that were then collapsed and dragged out the door; the resulting structures were windowless. All along the curve of one dark wall were banked brown cardboard boxes containing five hundred sheets each. Superoil's invisible minions had placed in the center of the hemisphere a long Masonite table, bland as a torturer's rack, and cartons of felt-tip pens. Bech never used felt-tip pens, preferring the manly gouge and sudden dry death of ballpoints. Nevertheless, he sat right down in his winter suit and ripped through a box, to see how it went.

It went like a breeze. Arrows, to be trimmed away by the binder, pointed to the area he must inscribe. Norma, as if still auditioning for the role of helpmate, pulled the sheets with a sweet deftness from underneath his wrists. Then they undressed—since he had last seen her naked, her body had softened, touchingly, and his body, too, wore a tallowish slump that appeared unfamiliar—and went out to swim in the lukewarm, late-afternoon sea. From its gentle surface the lowering sun struck coins of corporate happiness; Bech blessed Superoil as he floated, hairy belly up. The title of his next novel, after *Think Big* was in the bag, came to him: *Easy Money*. Or had Daniel Fuchs used it during the Depression? When he and Norma left their vast bath, the soft coral sand took deep prints from Bech's bare feet, as from those of a giant.

Wake, eat, swim, sun, sign, eat, sun, sign, drink, eat, dance, sleep. Thus their days passed. Their skins darkened. Bech became as swarthy as his Brazilian jacket photos. The stack of boxes of signed sheets slowly grew on the other side of the cement dome. They had to maintain an average of two thousand signatures a day. As Norma's tolerance for sun increased, she begrudged the time indoors, and seemed to Bech to be accelerating her pulling, so that more than once the concluding "h" got botched. "You're slowing down," she told him in self-defense, the third time this happened in one session.

"I'm just trying to give the poor bastards their buck-fifty's worth," he said. "Maybe you should pay attention to *me*, instead of trying to pull and read at the same time." She had taken to reading a novel at their signing table—a novel by, as it happened, a young writer who had, in the words of one critic, "made all previous American-Jewish writing look like so much tasteless matzo dough."

"I don't need to pay attention," she said. "I can hear

it now; there's a rhythm. Mm-diddle-um-*um*, boomity-boom. You lift your pen in the middle of 'Henry' and then hurry the 'Bech.' You love your first name and hate your last—why is that?"

"The 'B' is becoming harder and harder," he admitted. "Also, the 'e' and the 'c' are converging. Miss O'Dwyer at P.S. 87 tried to teach me the Palmer penmanship method once. She said you should write with your whole arm, not just your fingers."

"You're too old to change now; just keep doing it your way."

"I've decided she was right. These are ugly signatures. *Ugly*."

"For God's sake, Henry, don't try to make them works of art; all Superbooks wants is for you to keep touching pen to paper."

"Superbooks wants super signatures," he said. "At least they want signatures that show an author at peace with himself. Look at my big 'H's. They've turned into backward 'N's. And then the little 'h' at the end keeps tailing down. That's a sign of discouragement. Napoleon, you know, after Waterloo, every treaty he signed, his signature dragged down right off the page. The parchment."

"Well, you're not Napoleon, you're just an unemployed self-employed who's keeping me out of the sun."

"You'll get skin cancer. Relax. Eleven hundred more and we'll go have a piña colada."

"You're fussing over them, I can't stand it! You just *romped* through those early boxes."

"I was younger then. I didn't understand my signature so well. For being so short, it has a lot of ups and downs.

Suppose I was Robert Penn Warren. Suppose I was Sol-zhenitsyn."

"Suppose you were H. D., I'd still be sitting here in this damn dark igloo. You know, it's getting to my shoulders. The pauses between are the worst—the tension."

"Go out in the sun. Read your pimply genius. I'll be my own puller."

"Now you're trying to hurt my feelings."

"I'll be fine. I know my own rhythm."

"The Henry Bech backward crawl. I'll see this through if it kills us both."

He attempted a signature, hated the "nry," and slashed a big "X" across the sheet. "Your vibes are destroying me," he said.

"That was a dollar fifty," Norma said, standing in protest.

"Yeah, and here's the sales tax," Bech said, and X-ed out the preceding signature, whose jerky "ch" linkage had disturbed him as he did it, though he had decided to let it pass. He crumpled the sheet into a ball and hit her with it squarely between the two pieces of her bathing suit.

After this, when they sat down on opposite sides of the long table, fear of this quarrel's being repeated clotted their rapport. Fear of impotence seized his hand. The small digital muscles, asked to perform the same task thousands upon thousands of times, were rebelling. Sabotage appeared on the assembly line. Extra squiggles produced "Hennry," and the "B" of "Bech" would come out horribly cramped, like a symptom of a mental disease.

While the sun poured down, and the other resort guests could be heard tinkling and babbling at the thatched beach bar not far away, Bech would write "Henry" and forget what word came next. The space between his first and last name widened as some uncappable pressure welled up between them. The whole signature kept drifting outside the arrows, though he shoved with his brain while Norma tugged the stacks of sheets into repeated readjustments. Their daily quota fell below two thousand, to seventeen hundred, then to three boxes, and then they stopped counting boxes.

"We *must* sign them all here," Norma pleaded. "They're too heavy to take away with us." Their two weeks were drawing to a close, and the wall of unopened boxes seemed to grow, rustling, in the night. They sliced them open with a blade from Bech's razor; he cut his forefinger and had to pinch the pen through a Band-Aid. The pens themselves, so apparently identical at first, revealed large differences to his hypersensitive grasp, and as many as six had to be discarded before he found one that was not too light or heavy, whose flow and his were halfway congenial. Even so, one signature in five came out defective, while Norma groaned and tried to massage her own shoulders. "I think it's writer's cramp," she said.

"There's a paradox," he said. "You know, toward the end of his career Hogan would absolutely freeze over a one-foot putt."

"Don't make conversation," Norma begged. "Just inscribe."

The loudspeaking system strung through the palm trees interrupted its millionth rendition of "Yellow Bird" to announce his name. Over the phone in the manager's office, the man from Superoil said, "We figured you'd be a hundred-percent done by tomorrow, so we've arranged for a courier to jet in and ship the sheets to our bindery in Oregon."

"We've run into some snags," Bech told him. "Also, the pullers are restive."

The voice went a shade more hollow. "What percent would you say is still to be executed?"

"Hard to say. The boxes have grown big as freight cars. At first they were the size of matchboxes. Maybe there's ten left."

A silence. "Can you stonewall it?"

"I'm not sure that's the phrase. How about 'hot-dog it'?"

"The jet's been commissioned; it can't be cancelled. Do the best you can, and bring the rest back in your luggage."

"Luggage!" Norma scoffed, back at the igloo. "I'd just as soon try to pack a coral reef. And I re*fuse* to ruin my last full day here."

Bech worked all afternoon by himself, while she sauntered on the beach and fell in with a pair of scuba divers. "Jeff wanted me to go underwater with him, but I was scared our hoses would get tangled," she reported. "How many did you do?"

"Maybe a box. I kept getting dizzy." It was true; his signature had become a cataclysmic terrain of crags and abysses. His fingers traced the seismograph of a constant earthquake. Deep in the strata of time, a hot magma heaved. Who was this Henry Bech? What had led him up, up from his seat in his row in Miss O'Dwyer's class, to this impudent presumptive scrawl of fame? Her severe ghost mocked him every time an "e" collapsed or a "B" shrivelled at his touch.

Norma inspected his work. "These are wild," she said. "There's only one thing to do: get some piña coladas and stay up all night. I'm game."

"That makes one of us."

"You bastard. I've ruined my life waiting for you to do *some*thing and you're going to do *this*. Then that's it. This is the last thing I'll ever see you through."

"As Joan of Arc often said to the Dauphin," Bech said.

His dream-forgetting mechanism drew a merciful curtain over the events of that night. At one point, after the last trip to the bar had produced a bottle of rum and a six-pack of grape soda, his signature reached up from the page and tried to drag him down into it. Then he seemed to be pummelling Norma, but his fist sank in her slack belly as in muddy water. She plucked an arrow from an unsigned sheet and fended him off. The haggard dawn revealed one box still to be opened, and a tranquil sea dyed solid Day-Glo. They walked along the arc of beach holding inky hands. "Bech, Bech," the little waves whispered, mispronouncing the "ch." He and Norma fell asleep diagonally on the bed, amid sliced cardboard. The commotion at their louvered door woke them to a surge of parched nausea. Two black men were loading the boxes onto a trolley. The bundles of opened and resealed wrapping paper looked altogether strange, indecent, and perishable out in the air, among the stark morning verities of sky and sand and sea. Bathers gathered curiously about the pyramid, this monstrous accumulation hatched from their cement egg. To Bech's exhaustion and hangover was added a sensation of shame, the same shame he felt in bookstores, or after vomiting. One of the black men asked him, "This all there is, mon?"

"There's one more box," Bech admitted. For the first time in two weeks, a cloud covered the sun.

"Big jet from de state of Delaware at de airport waiting for Sea Breeze Taxi deliber all dese boxes," the other black man explained. Suddenly rain, in gleaming globular drops each big enough to fill a shot glass, began to fall. The onlookers in bathing suits scattered. The cardboard darkened. The ink would blur, the paper would wrinkle and return to pulp. The black men trundled away the mountain of Bech's signatures, promising to return for the last box.

In the dank igloo, Norma had placed the final sheaf of five hundred sheets, trim and pure, in the center of the table. She seated herself on her side, ready to pull. Groggily Bech sat down, under the dome drumming with the downpour. The arrows on the top sheet pointed inward. Clever female fingers slipped under a corner, alert to ease it away. The two San Poco taximen returned, their shirts sopping, and stood along one wall, silent with awe of the cultural ritual they were about to witness. Bech lifted a pen. All was poised, and the expectant blankness of the paper seemed an utter bliss to the author, as he gazed deep into the negative perfection to which his career had been brought. He could not even write his own name.

Bech Third-Worlds It

In Ghana, the Ambassador was sixty and slender and spunky, and wore a suit white as himself. He bade the driver on the road from Accra to Cape Coast stop at a village where a remarkable native sculpture with uncanny mimetic sympathy created in painted plaster an ornate, enigmatic tower. Green and pink, decorated with scrolls and pineapples, the tower, as solid inside as a piece of marzipan, was guarded by life-size plaster soldiers dressed in uniforms that combined and compounded the devices of half a dozen imperial uniforms. Out of pasty plaster faces they stared with alien blue eyes toward the sea whence, beginning with the Portuguese, the white men had come. The strange structure was weathering rapidly in these tropics. Its purpose, Bech imagined, was magical; but it was their ambassadorial limousine, as it roared into the village at the head of a procession of raised dust, a tiny American flag flapping on one fender, that had the magical effect: the villagers vanished. While the little cultural delegation stood there, on the soft dirt, in the hot sun—the Ambassador, mopping his pink and impressive face; Bech, nervously picking at an eyetooth with the nail of his little finger; the cultural attaché, a curly-haired, informative, worried man from Minnesota; his assistant, a lanky black female from Charlotte, North Carolina, coifed in the only Afro, as far as Bech could see, in all of Africa; and their driver, a gleaming Ghanaian a full head shorter than the rest of them—the village's inhabitants peeped from behind palms and out of oval doorways. Bech was reminded of how, in Korea, the North Korean soldiers skulked on their side of the truce zone, some with binoculars, some with defiant gestures. "Did we do something wrong?" Bech asked.

"Hell, no," the Ambassador said, with his slightly staggering excess of enthusiasm, like a ringmaster shouting to the far rows, "that's just the way the buggers act."

In Seoul, at a party held in a temple converted to an official banquet hall, a Japanese poet was led up to Bech by a translator. "I have long desired," the translator said, "to make the acquaintanceship of the honorable Henry Bech."

"Why?" Bech thoughtlessly asked. He was very tired, and tired of being polite in Asia.

There was, this rude monosyllable translated, a smiling, steady answer. The translator put it, "Your beautiful book *Travel Light* told us of Japan what to expect of the future." More Japanese, translated as "Young hooligans with faces of glass." This surely meant Bech's most famous apparition, the begoggled motorcyclists in his first, now venerated and wearisome, novel.

The poet in the kimono was leaning at a fixed angle. Bech perceived that his serenity was not merely ethnic; he was drunk. "And you," Bech asked through the translator, "what do *you* do?"

The answer came back as "I write many poems."

Bech felt near fainting. The jet lag built up over the Pacific was unshakable, and everywhere he went, a dozen photographers in identical gray suits kept blinding him. And Korean schoolgirls, in waxy pigtails and blue school uniforms, kept slipping him love letters in elevators. Two minutes off the airplane, he had been asked four times, "What are your impressions of Korea?"

Where was he? A thin ochre man in a silvery kimono was swaying before him, upheld by a chunky translator whose eyes were crossed in a fury of attention. "And what are your poems about?" Bech asked.

The answer was prompt. "Flogs," the translator said. The poet beamed.

"Frogs?" Bech said. "My goodness. *Many* poems about frogs?"

"Many."

"How many?"

No question was too inane, here in this temple, to receive an answer. The poet himself intervened to speak the answer, in proud English. "One hunnert twelve."

. . .

The Cape Coast Castle breasted the green Atlantic like a ship; the great stone deck of the old slave fort was paved with plaques testifying to the deaths, after a year or two of service here, of young British officers—dead of fever at twenty, twenty-two, twenty-five. "They thought that gin kept away malaria," the cultural attaché told him, "so everybody was reeling drunk most of the time. They died drunk. It must have been some show."

"Why did they come?" Bech asked, in his role as ambassador from the kingdom of stupid questions.

"Same reason they came to the States," the attaché said. "To get out from under. To get rich quick."

"Didn't they know"—Bech felt piqued, as if the plaques around him were a class of inattentive students —"they would die?"

"Dead men tell no tales," the Ambassador interrupted heartily, brandishing an imaginary whip. "They kept the bad news mum back home and told the poor buggers fool tales about black gold. That's what they used to call this hellhole. The Gold Coast."

The Ambassador's party went down to the dungeons. In one, a shrine seemed operative; bones, scraps of glass, burned-out candles, and fresh ash dirtied a slab of rock. In the deepest dungeon, a trough cut into the stone floor would have carried away body wastes and a passageway where the visitors now had to crouch once led the black captives, manacled, out to the ships and the New World. Bare feet had polished a path across the shelf of rough rock. Overhead, a narrow stone speaking-tunnel would have issued the commands of the captors. "Any white man come down in here," the Ambassador explained with loud satisfaction, "he'd be torn apart quicker'n a rabbit."

This grottolike historical site still somehow echoed with, even seemed still to smell of, the packed, fearful life it had contained.

"Leontyne Price was here a year ago," the cultural attaché said. "She really flipped out. She began to sing. She said she had to."

Bech glanced at the black girl from Charlotte, to see if she were flipping out. She was impassive, secretarial. She had been here before; it was on the Ghana tour. Yet she felt Bech's glance and suddenly, there in the dungeon dimness, gave it a dark, cool return. Can looks kill?

In Venezuela, the tallest waterfall in the world was hidden by clouds. The plane bumped down in a small green clearing and jauntily wheeled to the end of the airstrip. The pilot was devil-may-care, with a Cesar Romero mustache and that same Latin all-giving smile, under careful opaque eyes. Bech's guide was a languid young olive-skinned woman employed by the Creole Petroleum Corporation, or the government Ministry of Human Resources, or both. She struck Bech as attractive but untouchable. He followed her out of the plane into tropical air, which makes all things look close; the river that flowed from the invisible waterfall was audible on several sides of them. At the far edge of the clearing, miniature brown people were walking, half-naked, though some wore hats. There were perhaps eight of them, the children among them smaller but in no other way different; they moved single file, with the wooden dignity of old-fashioned toys, doubly dwarfed by the wall of green forest and the mountainous clouds of the moist, windy sky. "Who are they?" Bech asked.

"Indians," his lovely guide answered. Her English was flawless; she had spent years at the University of Michigan. But something Hispanic made her answers curter than a North American's would have been.

"Where are they going?"

"Nowhere. They are going precisely nowhere."

Her emphasis, he imagined, invited Bech to question deeper. "What are they thinking?" he asked.

The question was odd enough to induce a silky blink.

"They are wondering," said the *señorita* then, "who you are."

"They can see me?"

They had vanished, the Indians, into the forest by the river, like chips of pottery lost in grass. "Perfectly," she told him. "They can see you all too well."

The audience at Cape Coast grew restive during Bech's long address on "The Cultural Situation of the American Writer," and afterward several members of the audience, dressed in the colorful robes of spokesmen, leaped to their feet and asked combative questions. "Why," asked a small bespectacled man, his voice tremulous and orotund over the microphone, "has the gentleman speaking in representation of the United States not mentioned any black writers? Does he suppose, may I ask, that the situation of the black writers in his country partakes of the decadent and, may I say, uninteresting situation he has described?"

"Well," Bech began, "I think, yes, the American Negro has his share of our decadence, though maybe not a full share—"

"We have heard all this before," the man was going on, robed like a wizard, his lilting African English boomed by the amplifying system, "of your glorious Melville and Whitman, of their *Moby Dick*s and *Scarlet Letters*—what of Eldridge Cleaver and Richard Wright, what of Langston Hughes and Rufus Magee? Why have you not read to us pretty posies of their words? We beg you, Bech, tell us what you mean by this phrase"—a scornful pause—" 'American writer.' "

The noise from the crowd was rising. They seemed to be mostly schoolgirls, in white blouses and blue skirts, as in Korea, except that their skin was black and their pig-tails stood straight up from their heads, or lay in corn rows that must have taken hours to braid. "I mean," Bech said, "any person who simultaneously writes and holds American citizenship."

He had not meant this to be funny and found the wave of laughter alarming. Was it with him or against him?

In Korea, there was little laughter at his talk on "American Humor in Twain, Tarkington, and Thurber." Though Bech himself, reading aloud at the dais beside the bored Belgian chairman, repeatedly halted to get his own chuckles under control, an echo of them arose only from the American table of the conference—and these were contributed mostly, Bech feared, as tactical support. The only other noise in the vast pale-green room was the murmur of translation (into French, Spanish, Japanese, and Korean) leaking from earphones that bored Orientals had removed. Also, a yipping noise now and then escaped from the Vietnamese table. This table, labelled Vietnam though it represented the vanishing entity called South Vietnam, happened alphabetically to be adjacent to that of the United States, and, in double embarrassment, one of the delegates happened to be crazy. A long-faced man with copious black hair cut in a bowl shape, he crooned and doodled to himself throughout all speeches and rose always to make the same speech, a statement that in Vietnam for twenty years the humor had been bitter. Humor was the conference subject. Malaysian professors cracked Malaysian one-liners; the panel on Burmese scatology was very dignified. There was never much laughter, and none when Bech concluded with some deep thoughts on domestic confusion as the necessary underside of bourgeois order. "*Y a-t-il des questions?*" the chairman asked.

A young man, Asiatic, in floppy colorless shirt and slacks, stood up with fear splayed on his face and began to scream. Scream, no, he was intoning from sheets of paper held shaking in his hands. Fear spread to the faces of those around him who could understand. Bech picked up the headset before him on the dais and dialed for the English translation. There was none, and silence also gaped in French, in Spanish, in Japanese. To judge from the uplifted, chanting sounds, the young man was reciting poetry. Two policemen as young as he, their faces as smooth as their white helmets and as aloof from their bodies as the faces in Oriental prints, came and took the young man's arms. When he struggled and attempted to read on, to the end, Bech presumed, of a stanza, the policeman on his right arm neatly chopped him on the side of the neck, so his head snapped and the papers scattered. No one laughed. Bech was informed later that the young man was a Korean satiric poet.

In Kenya, on the stage at Nairobi, a note was passed to Bech, saying, *Crazy man on yr. right in beret, dont call on him for any question.* But when Bech's talk, which he had adjusted since Ghana to "Personal Impressions of the American Literary Scene," was finished and he had fielded or fluffed the obligatory pokes about racism, Vietnam, and the American loss in Olympic basketball, a young goateed African in a beret stepped forward to the edge of the stage and, addressing Bech, said, "Your books, they are weeping, but there are no tears."

On a stage, everything is hysterically heightened. Bech, blinded by lights, was enraptured by what seemed the beautiful justice of the remark. At last, he was meeting the critic who understood him. At last, he had been given an opportunity to express and expunge the embarrassment he felt here in the Third World. "I know," he confessed. "I would *like* there to be tears," he added, feeling craven as he said it.

Insanely, the youthful black face opposite him, with its

Pharaonic goatee, had produced instant tears; they gleamed on his cheeks as, with the grace of those beyond harm, of clowns and paupers and kings, he indicated the audience to Bech by a regal wave of his hand and spoke, half to them, half to him. His lilt was drier than the West African lilt, it was flavored by Arabic and savanna; the East Africans were a leaner and more thin-lipped race than that which had supplied the Americas with slaves. "The world," he began, and hung that ever-so-current bauble of a word in the space of their gathered silence with apparent utter confidence that meaning would come and fill it, "is a worsening place. There can be no great help in words. This white man, who is a Jew, has come from afar to give us words. They are good words. Is it words we need? Do we need his words? What shall we give him back? In the old days, we would give him back death. In the old days, we would give him back ivory. But in these days, such gifts would make the world a worse place. Let us give him back words. Peace." He bowed to Bech.

Bech lifted enough from his chair to bow back, answering, "Peace." There was heavy, relieved applause, as the young man was led away by a white guard and a black.

In Caracas, the rich Communist and his elegant French wife had Bech to dinner to admire their Henry Moore. The Moore, a reclining figure of fiercely scored bronze —art seeking to imitate nature's patient fury—was displayed in an enclosed green garden where a floodlit fountain played and bougainvillaea flowered. The drinks —Scotch, Cointreau—materialized on glass tables. Bech wanted to enjoy the drinks, the Moore, the beauty of rich enclosure, the paradox of political opinion, but he was still unsettled by the flight from Canaima, where he had seen the tiny Indians disappear. The devil-may-care pilot had wanted to land at the unlighted military airfield in the middle of the city rather than at the international airport along the coast, and other small planes, also devil-may-care, kept dropping in front of him, racing with the fall of dusk, so he kept pulling back on the controls and cursing, and the plane would wheel, and the tin slums of the Caracas hillsides would flood the tipped windows— vertiginous surges of mosaic.

"*¡Caramba!*" the *escritor norteamericano* wanted to exclaim, but he was afraid of mispronouncing. He was pleased to perceive, through the surges of his terror, that his cool guide was terrified also. Her olive face looked aged, blanched. Her great silky eyelids closed in nausea or prayer. Her hand groped for his, her long fingernails scraping. Bech held her hand. He would die with her. The plane dived and smartly landed, under a romantic full moon just risen in the postcard-purple night sky above Monte Avila.

The Ambassador held a dinner for Bech and the Ghanaian elite. They were the elite under this regime, had been the elite under Nkrumah, would be the elite under the next regime. The relative positions within the elite varied, however; one slightly demoted man, with an exquisite Oxford accent, got drunk and told Bech and the women at their end of the table about walking behind Nkrumah in a procession. In those days (and no doubt in these), the elite had carried guns. "Quite without warning or any tangible provocation," the man told Bech, as gin-enriched sweat shone from his face as from a basalt star, "I was visited by this overpowering urge to kill him. Over*powering*—my palm was itching, I could feel the little grid of the revolver handle in my fingers, I focused hypnotically upon the precise spot, in the center of his occiput, where the bullet would enter. He had become a tyrant. Isn't that so, ladies?"

There was a soft, guarded tittering of agreement from the Ghanaian women. They were magnificent, Ghanaian women, from mammy wagon to Cabinet post, fertile and hopeful, wrapped in their sumptuous gowns and turbans. Bech wanted to repose forever, in the candlelight, amid these women, like a sultan amid so many pillows. Women and death and airplanes: there was a comfortable triangulation there, he drowsily perceived.

"The urge became irresistible," his informant was continuing. "I was wrestling with a veritable demon; sweat was rolling from me as from one about to vomit. I had to speak. It happened that I was walking beside one of his bodyguards. I whispered to him, 'Sammy. I want to shoot him.' I had to tell someone or I would have done it. I wanted him to prevent me, perhaps—who knows the depths of the slave mentality?—even to shoot me, before I committed sacrilege. You know what he said to me? He turned to me, this bodyguard, six foot two at the minimum, and solemnly said, 'Jimmy, me, too. But not now. Not yet. Let's wait.' "

In Lagos, they were sleeping in the streets. Returning in a limousine from a night club where he had learned to do the high-life (his instructress's waist like a live, slow snake in his hands), Bech saw the bodies stretched on the pavements, within the stately old British colonnades, under the street lamps, without blankets. Seen thus, people make a bucolic impression, of a type of animal, a hairless, especially peaceful type, performing one of the five acts essential to its existence. The others are: eating, drinking, breathing, and fornicating.

In Seoul, the prostitutes wore white. They were young girls, all of them, and in the white dresses, under their delicate parasols, they seemed children gathered along the walls of the hotels, waiting for a bus to take them to their first Communion. In Caracas, the whores stood along the main streets between the diagonally parked cars so that Bech had the gustatory impression of a drive-in restaurant blocks long, with the carhops allowed to choose their own uniforms, as long as they showed lots of leg, in several delicious flavors.

In Egypt, the beggars had sores and upturned, blind eyes; Bech felt they were gazing upward to their reward and sensed through them the spiritual pyramid, the sacred hierarchy of suffering that modern man struggles with nightmare difficulty to invert and to place upon a solid material base of sense and health and plenty. On an island in the Nile, the Royal Cricket Club flourished under new management; the portly men playing bowls and sipping gin were a shade or two darker than the British, but mannerly and jubilant. The bowling greens were level and bright, the gin was Beefeater's, the laughter of sportsmanship ricocheted, it was jolly, jolly. Bech was happy here. He was not happy everywhere, in the Third World.

A friend had fought in Korea and had told Bech, without rancor, that the whole country smelled of shit. Alighting from the plane, Bech discovered it to be true: a gamy, muddy smell swept toward him. That had been his first impression, which he had suppressed when the reporters asked for it.

As the audience in Cape Coast politely yielded up a scattered, puzzled applause, Bech turned to the Ambassador and said, "Tough questions."

The Ambassador, whose white planter's suit lacked only the wide-brimmed hat and the string tie, responded with a blast of enthusiasm. "Those weren't tough questions, those were kid-glove questions. Standard stuff. These buggers are soft; that's why they made good slaves. Before they sent me here, I was in Somaliland; the Danakil—now, those are buggers after my own heart. Kill you for a dime, for a nickel-plated spoon. Hell, kill you for the fun of it. Hated to leave. Just as I was learning the damn language. Full of grammar, Dankali."

Tanzania was eerie. The young cultural attaché was frighteningly with it, equally enthusiastic about the country's socialism and its magic. "So this old guy wrote the name of the disease and my brother's name on the skin of the guava and it *sank right in*. You could see the words moving *into the center*. I tried writing on a guava and I couldn't even make a mark. Sure enough, weeks later I get a letter from him saying he felt a lot better suddenly. And if you figure in the time change, it was *that very day*."

They kept Bech's profile low; he spoke not in a hall but in a classroom, at night, and then less spoke than deferentially listened. The students found decadent and uninteresting Proust, Joyce, Shakespeare, Sartre, Hemingway—Hemingway, who had so enjoyed coming to Tanganyika and killing its kudu and sitting by its campfires getting drunk and pontifical—and Henry James. Who, then, Bech painfully asked, *did* measure up to the exacting standards that African socialism had set for literature? The answering silence lengthened. Then the brightest boy, the most militant and vocal, offered, "Jack London," and rubbed his eyes. He was tired, Bech realized. Bech was tired. Jack London was tired. Everything in the world was tired, except fear—fear and magic.

Alone on the beach in Dar es Salaam, where he had been warned against going alone, he returned to the sand after trying to immerse himself in the milky, shoal-beshallowed Indian Ocean and found his wristwatch gone. There was nothing around him but palms and a few rocks. And no footprints but his own led to his blanket. Yet the watch was gone from where he had distinctly placed it; he remembered its tiny threadlike purr in his ear as he lay with his back to the sun. It was not the watch, a drugstore Timex bought on upper Broadway. It was the fear he minded, the terror of the palms, the rocks, the pale, unsatisfactory ocean, his sharp small shadow, the mocking emptiness all around. The Third World was a vacuum that might suck him in, too, along with his wristwatch and the words on the skin of the guava.

At the center of a panel of the Venezuelan elite, Bech discussed "The Role of the Writer in Society." Spanish needs more words, evidently, than even English to say something, so the intervals of translation were immense. The writer's duty to society, Bech had said, was simply to tell the truth, however strange, small, or private his truth appeared. During the eternity while the translator, a plump, floridly gesturing woman, rendered this into the microphone, one panelist kept removing and replacing his glasses fussily and the rich Communist studied his own right hand as if it had been placed by an officious waiter on the table—square, tan, cuffed in white and ringed in gold. But what, the man with the restless spectacles was at last allowed to ask, of Dreiser and Jack London, of Steinbeck and Sinclair Lewis—what has happened in the United States to their noble tradition of social criticism?

It's become sexual display, Bech could have said; but he chose to answer in terms of Melville and Henry James, though he was weary, weary to death of dragging their large, obliging, misshapen reputations around the globe, rag dummies in which the stuffing had long ago slipped and dribbled out the seams. Words, words. As Bech talked, and his translatress feverishly scribbled notes upon his complicated gist, young Venezuelans—students—not too noisily passed out leaflets among the audience and scattered some on the table. The Communist glanced at one, put it face down on the table, and firmly rested his handsome, unappetizing hand upon the now blank paper. Bech looked at the one that slid to a stop at the base of his microphone. It showed himself, huge-nosed, as a vulture with striped and starred wings, perched on a tangle of multicolored little bodies; beneath the caricature ran the capitalized words INTELECTUAL REACCIONARIO, IMPERIALISTA, ENEMIGO DE LOS PUEBLOS.

The English words "Rolling Stone" leaped out at him. Some years ago in New York City he had irritably given an interviewer for *Rolling Stone* a statement, on Vietnam, to the effect that, challenged to fight, a country big enough has to fight. Also he had said that, having visited the Communist world, he could not share radical illusions about it and could not wish upon Vietnamese peasants a system he would not wish upon himself. Though it was what he honestly thought, he was sorry he had said it. But then, in a way, he was sorry he had ever said anything, on anything, ever. He had meddled with sublime silence. There was in the world a pain concerning which God has set an example of unimpeachable no comment. These realizations took the time of one short, not even awkward pause in his peroration about ironic points of light; bravely, he droned on, wondering when the riot and his concomitant violent death would begin.

But the Venezuelan students, having distributed their flier, stood back, numbed by the continuing bombardment of North American pedantry, and even gave way, murmuring uncertainly, when the panel wound down and Bech was escorted by the USIS men and the rich Communist from the hall. They looked, the students, touchingly slim, neat, dark-eyed, and sensitive—the fineness of their skin and hair especially struck him, as if the furrier eye of his uncle Mort had awakened within him and he were appraising pelts. By the doorway, he passed close enough to reach out and touch them. Had he known Spanish, Bech might have told these youngsters how grateful he, like one of those dragons in Spenser craving to be eliminated from the lists of evil, was for their attempt to slay him.

He lived. Outdoors, in the lustrous, shuffling tropical night, the Communist writer stayed with him until the USIS men had flagged a taxi and, in response to Bech's protestations of gratitude (for being his bodyguard, for showing him his Moore), gave him a correct, cold handshake. A rich radical and a poor reactionary: natural allies, both resenting it.

To quiet Bech's fear, the State Department underlings took him to a Caracas tennis tournament, where, under bright lights, a defected Czech beat a ponytailed Swede. But his dread did not lift until, next morning, having signed posters and books for all the wives and cousins of the embassy personnel, he was put aboard the Pan Am jet at the Maiquetía airport. His government had booked him first class. He ordered a drink as soon as the seat-belt sign went off. The stewardess had a Texas accent and a cosmetically flat stomach. She smiled at him. She blamed him for nothing. He might die with her. The sun above the boundless cloud fields hurled through the free bourbon a golden arc that shuddered beside the plastic swizzle stick, upon the plastic tray. In Korea, the girls in school uniforms would slip him notes on blue-lined paper reading, *Derest Mr Bech Mr Kim our teacher assined your stori on being Jewsh in English clas it was my favrite ever I think you very famus over the world I love you.* In Nigeria, the woman teaching him the high-life had reached out and placed two firm black hands gently upon his hips, to settle him down: he had been doing a jumpy, aggressive frug to this different, subtler beat. In the air, the 747 hit some chop and jiggled, but stayed aloft. Not a drop of his golden drink spilled. He vowed never to Third-World it again, unless somebody asked him to.

Australia and Canada

CLEAN STRAIGHT STREETS. Cities whose cores are not blighted but innocently bustling. Anglo-Saxon citizens, British once removed, striding long-legged and unterrorized out of a dim thin past into a future as likely as any. Empty territories rich in minerals. Stately imperial government buildings. Parks where one need not fear being mugged. Bech in his decline went anywhere but had come to prefer safe places.

The invitation to Canada was to Toronto, to be interviewed, as Henry Bech, the exquisitely unprolific author, on the television program *Vanessa Views*. Vanessa was a squat woman with skin like orange cheesecloth, who nevertheless looked, on a twenty-three-inch screen, if not beautiful, alive. "It's all in the eyes," she explained. "The people with deep sockets do terribly. To project to the camera, you must have eyes set forward in your head. If your eyes turn inward, the viewers turn right off."

"Suppose your eyes," Bech asked, "turn toward each other?"

Vanessa refused to pick it up as a joke, though a female voice behind the lights and cameras laughed. "You are an author," Vanessa told him sternly. "You don't have to project. Indeed, you shouldn't. Viewers distrust the ones who do."

The two of them were caught in the curious minute before airtime. Bech, practiced rough-smoothie that he was, chatted languidly, fighting down the irreducible nervousness, a floating and rising sensation as if he were, with every second ticked from the huge studio clock, being inflated. His hands prickled, swelling; he looked at his palms and they seemed to have no wrinkles. His face felt stiff, having been aromatically swabbed with something like that strange substance with which one was supposed, thirty years ago, to color oleomargarine and thereby enhance the war effort. The female who had laughed behind the lights, he saw, was the producer, a leggy girl pale as untinted oleo, with nostrils reddened by a cold, and lifeless, pale hair she kept flicking back with the hand not holding her handkerchief. Named Glenda, she appeared harried by her own efficiency, which she refused to acknowledge, brushing aside her directives to the cameramen as soon as she issued them. Like himself, Bech felt, she had been cast by life into a role it amused her not quite to fill.

Whereas his toadlike interviewer, whose very warts were telegenic, inhaled and puffed herself way up; she was determined to fill this attenuated nation from coast to coast. The seconds waned into single digits on the studio clock and a muffled electronic fuss beyond the lights clicked into gear and Bech's pounding heart bloated as if to choke him. Vanessa began to talk. Then, miracle that never failed, so did he.

He talked into the air. Even without the bright simulacrum of his head and shoulders gesticulating in the upper-left corner of his vision, where the monitor hung like an illuminated initial on a page of shadowy manuscript, Bech could feel the cameras licking his image up and flinging it, quick as light, from Ontario to British Columbia. He touched his nose to adorn a pensive pause, and the gesture splashed onto the shores of the Maritime Provinces and fell as silver snow upon the barren Yukon. As he talked, he marvelled at his words as much as at the electronic marvel that broadcast them; for, just as this broadcasting was an airy and flattering shell upon the terrestrial, odorous, confused man who physically occupied a plastic chair and a few cubic feet of space in this tatty studio, so his words were a shell, an unreal umbrella, above his kernel of real humanity, the more or less childish fears and loves that he wrote out of, when he wrote. On the monitor now, while his throaty interviewer described his career with a "voice-over," stills of his books were being flashed, and from their jackets photographs of Bech—big-eared and combative, a raw youth, on the flap of *Travel Light*; a few years older on *Brother Pig*, his hair longer, his gaze more guarded and, it seemed to Bech in the microsecond of its exposure, illicitly conspiratorial, seeking to strike up a mutually excusatory relationship with the reader; a profile, frankly and vapidly Bachrachian, from his collection of essays;

and, wizened if not wiser, pouchy and classy as a golf bag, his face, haloed by wild wool that deserved to belong to a Kikuyu witch doctor, from the back of his "big" novel, which had been, a decade ago, jubilantly panned. Bech realized, viewing the montage, that as his artistic powers had diminished he had come to look more and more like an artist. Then, an even older face, the shocking face of a geezer, of a shambler, with a furtive wit waiting to twitch the licked and criminal lips, flashed onto the screen, and he realized it was he, he as of this moment, on camera, live. The talking continued, miraculously.

Afterward, the producer of the show emerged from behind the cables and the cameras, told him he was wonderful, and, the day being fair, offered to take him for a tour of the city. He had three hours before a scheduled dinner with a Canadian poet who had fenced with Cocteau and an Anglican priest who had prepared a concordance of Bech's fiction. Glenda flicked back her hair absent-mindedly; Bech scanned her face for a blip marking how far she expected him to go. Her eyes were an even gray shallowly backed by a neutral Northern friendliness. He accepted.

In Australia, the tour of Sydney was conducted by two girls, Hannah, the dark and somber prop girl for the TV talk show on which he had been a seven-minute guest (along with an expert on anthrax; a leader of the Western Australia secessionist movement; a one-armed surviver of a shark attack; and an aborigine protest painter), plus Moira, who lived with Hannah and was an instructor in the economics of underdevelopment. The day was not fair. A downpour hit just as Hannah drove her little Subaru to the Opera House, so they did not get out but admired the world-famous structure from the middle distance. A set of sails had been the architect's metaphor; but it looked to Bech more like a set of fish mouths about to nibble something. Him, perhaps. He gave Hannah permission to drive away. "It's too bad," Moira said from the back seat, "the day is so rotten. The whole thing is covered in a white ceramic that's gorgeous in the sun."

"I can picture it," Bech lied politely. "Inside, does it give a feeling of grandeur?"

"No," said Hannah.

"It's all rather tedious bits and pieces," Moira elaborated. "We fired the Dane who did the outside and finished the inside ourselves."

The two girls' life together, Bech guessed, contained a lot of Moira's elaboration, around the other's dark and somber core. Hannah had moved toward him, after the show, as though by some sullen gravitational attraction such as the outer planets feel for the sun. He was down under, Bech told himself; his volume still felt displaced by an eternity in airplanes. But Hannah's black eyes had no visible backs to them. Down, in, down, they said.

She drove to a cliffy point from which the harbor, the rain lifting, gleamed like silver long left unpolished. Sydney, Moira explained, loved its harbor and embraced it like no other city in the world, not even San Francisco. She had been in San Francisco once, on her way to

Afghanistan. Hannah had not been anywhere since leaving Europe at the age of three. She was Jewish, said her eyes, and her glossy, tapered fingers. She drove them down to Bondi Beach, and they removed their six shoes to walk on the soaked sand. The tops of Bech's fifty-year-old feet looked white as paper to him, cheap paper, as if his feet amounted to no more than the innermost lining of his shoes. The girls ran ahead and challenged him to a broad-jump contest. He won. Then, in the hop, step, and jump, his heart felt pleasantly as if it might burst, down here, where death was not real. Blond surfers, wet-suited, were tumbling in with the dusk; a chill wind began sweeping the cloud tatters away. Hannah at his side said, "That's one reason for wearing a bra."

"What is?" Moira asked, hearing no response from Bech.

"Look at my nipples. I'm cold."

Bech looked down; indeed, the woman wore no bra and her erectile tissue had responded to the drop in temperature. The rare sensation of a blush caked his face, which still wore its television makeup. He lifted his eyes from Hannah's sweater and saw that, like fancy underpants, the entire beach was frilled, with pink and lacy buildings. Sydney, the girls explained, as the tour continued from Bondi to Woollahra to Paddington to Surry Hills and Redfern, abounds in ornate ironwork shipped in as ballast from England. The oldest buildings were built by convicts: barracks and forts of a pale stone cut square and set solid, as if by the very hand of rectitude.

In Toronto, the sight Glenda was proudest to show him was the City Hall, two huge curved skyscrapers de-

signed by a Finn. But what moved Bech, with their
intimations of lost time and present innocence, were the
great Victorian piles, within the university and along
Bloor Street, that the Canadians, building across the lake
from grimy grubbing America, had lovingly erected—
brick valentines posted to a distant, unamused queen.
Glenda talked about the city's community of American
draft evaders and the older escapees, the families who
were fleeing to Canada post-Vietnam, because life in the
United States had become, what with race and corruption and pressure and trash, impossible.

Flicking back her pale hair as if to twitch it into life,
Glenda asssumed Bech agreed with her and the exiles,
and so a side of him lackadaisically did; but another side,
his ugly patriotism, bristled as she chattered on about his
country's sins and her own blameless land's Balkaniza-
tion by the money that, even in its death throes, American capitalism was flinging north. Hearing this, Bech felt
the pride of vicarious power—he who lived cowering on
drug-ridden West Ninety-ninth Street, avoiding both the
venture of marriage, though his suburban mistress was
more than ready, and the venture of print, though his
editor, dear old Ned Clavell, from his deathbed in the
Harkness Pavilion had begged him to come up at least
with a memoir. While Glenda talked, Bech felt like
something immense and confusedly vigorous about to
devour something dainty. He feigned assent and praised
the new architecture booming along the rectitudinal
streets, because he believed that this woman—her body a
hand's-breadth away on the front seat of a Canadian Ford
—liked him, liked even the whiff of hairy savagery about

him; his own body wore the chill, the numb expectancy all over his skin, that foretold a sexual conquest.

He interrupted her. "Power corrupts," he said. "The powerless should be grateful."

She looked over dartingly. "Do I sound smug to you?"

"No," he lied. "But then, you don't seem powerless to me, either. Quite masterful, the way you run your TV crew."

"I enjoy it, is the frightening thing. You were lovely, did I say that? So giving. Vanessa can be awfully obvious in her questions."

"I didn't mind. You do it and it flies over all those wires and vanishes. Not like writing, that sits there and gives you that Gorgon stare."

"What are you writing now?"

"As I said to Vanessa. A novel with the working title *Think Big*."

"I thought you were joking. How big is it?"

"It's bigger than I am."

"I doubt that."

I love you. It would have been easy to say, he was so grateful for her doubt, but his sensation of numbness, meaning love was at hand, had not yet deepened to total anesthesia. "I love," he told her, turning his face to the window, "your sensible, pretty city."

"Loved it," Bech said of his tour of Sydney. "Want to drop me at the hotel?"

"No," Hannah said.

"You must come home and let us give you a bite," Moira elaborated. "Aren't you a hungry lion? Peter said he'd drop around and that would make four."

"Peter?"

"He has a degree in forestry," Moira explained.

"Then what's he doing here?"

"He's left the forest for a while," Hannah said.

"Which of you . . . knows him?" Bech asked, jealously, hesitantly.

But his hesitation was slight compared with theirs; both girls were silent, waiting for the other to speak. At last Hannah said, "We sort of share him."

Moira added, "He was mine, but Hannah stole him and I'm in the process of stealing him back."

"Sounds fraught," Bech said; the clipped Australian lilt was already creeping into his enunciation.

"No, it's not so bad," Moira said into his ear. "The thing that saves the situation is, after he's gone, we have each other. We're amazingly compatible."

"It's true," Hannah somberly pronounced, and Bech felt jealous again, of their friendship, or love if it were love. He had nobody. Flaubert without a mother. Bouvard without a Pécuchet. Even Bea, whose sad suburban life had become a continuous prayer for him to marry her, had fallen silent, the curvature of the earth interceding.

They had driven in the darkness past palm-studded parks and golf courses, past shopping streets, past balconies of iron lace, into a region of dwarf row houses, spruced up and painted pastel shades: Bohemia salvaging another slum. Children were playing in the streets and called to their car, recognizing Hannah. Bech felt safe. Or would have but for Peter, the thought of him, the man from the forest, on whose turf the aged lion was daring to intrude.

The section of Toronto where Glenda drove him, proceeding raggedly uphill, contained large homes, British in their fussy neo-Gothic brickwork but New World in their untrammelled scale and large lawns—lawns dark as overinked etchings, shadowed by great trees strayed south from the infinite forests of the north. Within one of these miniature castles, a dinner party had been generated. The Anglican priest who had prepared the concordance asked him if he were aware of an unusual recurrence in his work of the adjectives *lambent, untrammelled, porous, jubilant,* and *recurrent.* Bech said no, he was not aware, and that if he could have thought of other adjectives, he would have used them instead— that a useful critical distinction should be made, perhaps, between recurrent imagery and authorial stupidity; that it must have taken him, the priest, an immense amount of labor to compile such a concordance, even of an *oeuvre* so slim. Ah, not really, was the answer: the texts had been readied by the seminarians in his seminar in post-Christian kerygmatics, and the collation and printout had been achieved by a scanning computer in twelve minutes flat.

The writer who had cried *"Touché!"* to Cocteau was ancient and ebullient. His face was as red as a mountain-climber's, his hair fine as thistledown. He chastened Bech with his air of the Twenties, when authors were happy in their trade and boisterous in plying it. As the whiskey and wine and cordials accumulated, the old saint's arm (in a shimmering grape-colored shirt) frequently encircled Glenda's waist and bestowed a paternal hug; later, when she and Bech were inspecting together (the glaze of alcohol intervening so that he felt he was bending above a glass museum case) a collector's edition of the Canadian's most famous lyric, *Pines*, Glenda, as if to "rub off" on the American the venerable poet's blessing, caressed him somehow with her entire body, while two of their four hands held the booklet. Her thigh rustled against his, a breast gently tucked itself into the crook of his arm, his entire skin went blissfully porous, he felt as if he were toppling forward. "Time to go?" he asked her.

"Soon," Glenda answered.

Peter was not inside the girls' house, though the door was open and his dirty dishes were stacked in the sink. Bech asked, "Does he *live* here?"

"He eats here," Hannah said.

"He lives right around the corner," Moira elaborated. "Shall I go fetch him?"

"Not to please me," Bech said; but she was gone, and the rain recommenced. The sound drew the little house snug into itself—the worn Oriental rugs, the rows of books about capital and underdevelopment, the New Guinean and Afghan artifacts on the wall, all the frail bric-a-brac of women living alone, in nests without eggs.

Hannah poured them two Scotches and tried to roll a joint. "Peter usually does this," she said, fumbling, spil-

ling. Bech as a child had watched Westerns in which cow-
pokes rolled cigarettes with one hand and a debonair lick.
But his efforts at imitation were so clumsy that Hannah
took the paper and the marijuana back from him and
made of these elements a plump-tongued packet, a little
white dribbling piece of pie, which they managed to
smoke, amid many sparks. Bech's throat between sips of
liquor burned. Hannah put on a record. The music went
through its grooves, over and over. The rain continued
steady, though his consciousness of it was intermittent.
At some point in the rumpled stretches of time, she
cooked an omelet. She talked about her career, her life,
the man she had left to live with Moira, Moira, herself.
Her parents were from Budapest; they had been refugees
in Portugal during World War II, and when it was over,
only Australia would let them in. An Australian Jewess,
Bech thought, swallowing to ease his burned throat. The
concept seemed unappraisably near and far, like that of
Australia itself. He was here, but it was there, a world's
fatness away from his empty, sour, friendly apartment at
Riverside and Ninety-ninth. He embraced her and they
seemed to bump together like two clappers in the same
bell. She was fat, solid. Her body felt in his arms hinge-
less; she was one of those wooden peasant dolls, containing congruent dolls, for sale in Slavic Europe, where he
had once been, and where she had been born. He asked
her among their kisses, which came and went in his consciousness like the sound of the rain, and which travelled
circularly in grooves like the music, if they should wait
up for Peter and Moira.

"No," Hannah said.

If Moira had been there, she would have elaborated, but she wasn't and therefore didn't.

"Shall I come up?" Bech asked. For Glenda lived on the top floor of a Toronto castle a few blocks' walk—a swim, through shadows and leaves—from the house they had left.

"All I can give you," she said, "is coffee."

"Just what I need, fortuitously," he said. "Or should I say lambently? Jubilantly?"

"You poor dear," Glenda said. "Was it so awful for you? Do you have to go to parties like that every night?"

"Most nights," he told her, "I'm scared to go out. I sit home reading Dickens and watching Nixon. And nibbling pickles. And picking quibbles. Recurrently."

"You do need the coffee, don't you?" she said, still dubious. Bech wondered why. Surely she was a sure thing. That shimmering body touch. Her apartment snuggled under the roof, bookcases and lean lamps looking easy to tip among the slanting walls. In a far room he glimpsed a bed, with a feathery Indian bedspread and velour pillows. Glenda, as firmly as she directed cameramen, led him the other way, to a small front room claustrophobically lined with books. She put on a record, explaining it was Gordon Lightfoot, Canada's own. A sad voice, gentle to no clear purpose, imitated American country blues. Glenda talked about her career, her life, the man she had been married to.

"What went wrong?" Bech asked. Marriage and death fascinated him: he was an old-fashioned novelist in this.

She wanly shrugged. "He got too dependent. I was being suffocated. He was terribly nice, a truly nice person. But all he would do was sit and read and ask me questions about my feelings. These books, they're mostly his."

"You seem tired," Bech said, picturing the feathery bed.

She surprised him by abruptly volunteering, "I have something wrong with my corpuscles, they don't know what it is, I'm having tests. But I'm out of whack. That's why I said I could offer you only coffee."

Bech was fascinated, flattered, relieved. Sex needed participation, illness needed only a witness. A loving witness. Glenda was dear and directorial in her movement as she rose and flicked back her hair and turned the record over. The movement seemed to generate a commotion on the stairs, and then a key in the lock and a brusque masculine shove on the door. She turned a notch paler, staring at Bech; the pink part of her nose stood out like an exclamation point. Too startled to whisper, she told Bech, "It must be *Peter*."

Downstairs, more footsteps than two entered the little house, and from the grumble of a male voice, Bech deduced that Moira had at last returned with Peter. Hannah slept, her body filling the bed with a protective turnipy warmth he remembered from Brooklyn kitchens. The couple below them bumbled, clattered, tittered, put on a record. It was a Chilean flute record Hannah had played for him earlier—music shrill, incessant, searching, psychedelic. This little white continent, abandoned at the foot of Asia, looked to the New World's west coasts for culture, for company. California clothes, Andean flutes. "My pale land," he had heard an Australian poet recite; and from airplanes it was, indeed, a pale land, speckled and colorless, a Wyoming with a seashore. A continent as lonely as the planet. Peter and Moira played the record again and again; otherwise, they were silent downstairs, deep in drugs or fucking. Bech got up and groped lightly across the surface of Hannah's furniture for Kleenex or lens tissue or anything tearable to stuff into his ears. His fingers came to a paperback book and he thought the paper might be cheap enough to wad. Tearing off two corners of the title page, he recognized by the dawning light the book as one of his own, the Penguin *Brother Pig*, with that absurdly literal cover, of a grinning pig, as if the novel were *Animal Farm* or *Charlotte's Web*. The paper crackling and cutting in his ears, he returned to the bed. Beside him, stately Hannah, half-covered and unconscious, felt like a ship, her breathing an engine, her lubricated body steaming toward the morning, her smokestack nipples relaxed in passage. The flute music stopped. The world stopped turning. Bech counted to ten, twenty, thirty in silence, and his consciousness had begun to disintegrate when a man laughed and the Chilean flute, and the pressure in Bech's temples, resumed.

"This is Peter Syburg," Glenda said. "Henry Bech."

"*Je sais, je sais bien,*" Peter said, shaking Bech's hand with the painful vehemence of the celebrity-conscious. "I saw your gig on the tube. Great. You talked a blue streak and didn't tip your hand once. What a con job.

Cool. I mean it. The medium is *you*, man. Hey, that's a compliment. Don't look that way."

"I was just going to give him coffee," Glenda interposed.

"How about brandy?" Bech asked. "Suddenly I need my spirits fortified."

"Hey, don't go into your act," Peter said. "I *like* you."

Peter was a short man, past thirty, with thinning ginger hair and a pumpkin's gat-toothed grin. He might have even been forty; but a determined retention of youth's rubberiness fended off the possibility. He flopped into a canvas sling chair and kept crossing and recrossing his legs, which were so short he seemed to Bech to be twiddling his thumbs. Peter was a colleague of sorts, based at the CBC office in Montreal, and used Glenda's apartment here when she was in Montreal, as she often was, and vice versa. Whether he used Glenda when she was in Toronto was not clear to Bech; less and less was. Less and less the author understood how people lived. Such cloudy episodes as these had become his only windows into other lives. He wanted to go, but his going would be a retreat—Montcalm wilting before Wolfe's stealthy ascent. He had a bit more brandy instead. He found himself embarked on one of those infrequent experiments in which, dispassionate as a scientist bending metal, he tested his own capacity. He felt himself inflating, as before television exposure, while the brandy flowed on and Peter asked him all the questions not even Vanessa had been pushy enough to pose ("What's happened to you and Capote?" "What's the timer makes you Yanks burn out so fast?" "Ever thought of trying television scripts?") and expatiating on the wonders of the McLuhanite world in which he, Peter, with his thumb-like legs and berry-bright eyes, moved as a successful creature, while he, Bech, was picturesquely extinct. Glenda flicked her pale hair and studied her hands and insulted her out-of-whack corpuscles with cigarettes. Bech was happy. One more brandy, he calculated, would render him utterly immobile, and Peter would be displaced. His happiness was not even punctured when the two others began to talk to each other in Canadian French, about calling a taxi to take him away.

"*Taxi, non,*" Bech exclaimed, struggling to rise. "*Marcher, oui. Je pars, maintenant. Vous le regretterez, quand je suis disparu. Au revoir, cher Pierre.*"

"You can't walk it, man. It's miles."

"Try me, you post-print punk," Bech said, putting up his hairy fists.

Glenda escorted him to the stairs and down them, one by one; at the foot, she embraced him, clinging to him as if to be rendered fertile by osmosis. "I thought he was in Winnipeg," she said. "I want to have your baby."

"Easy does it," Bech wanted to say. The best he could do was, "*Facile le fait.*"

Glenda asked, "Will you ever come back to Toronto?"

"*Jamais,*" Bech said, "*jamais, jamais,*" and the magical word, so true of every moment, of every stab at love, of every step on ground you will not walk again, rang in his mind all the way back to the hotel. The walk was generally downhill. The curved lights of the great city hall guided him. There was a forested ravine off to his left, and a muffled river. And stars. And block after block of substantial untroubled emptiness. He expected to be mugged, or at least approached. In his anesthetized state, he would have welcomed violence. But in those miles he met only blinking stop lights and impassive architecture. *And they call this a city*, Bech thought scornfully. *In New York, I would have been killed six times over and my carcass stripped of its hubcaps.*

The cries of children playing woke him. The sound of the flute at last had ceased. Last night's pleasure had become straw in his mouth; the woman beside him seemed a larger sort of dreg. Her eyelids fluttered, as if in response to the motions of his mind. It seemed only polite to reach for her. The children beneath the window cheered.

Next morning, in Toronto, Bech shuffled, footsore, to the Royal Ontario Museum and admired the Chinese urns and the totem poles and sent a postcard of a carved walrus tusk to Bea and her three children.

Downstairs, in Sydney, Moira was up, fiddling with last night's dishes and whistling to herself. Bech recognized the tune. "Where's Peter?" he asked.

"He's gone," she said. "He doesn't believe you exist. We waited up hours for you last night and you never came home."

"We *were* home," Hannah said.

"Oh, it dawned on us finally." She elaborated: "Peter was so moody I told him to leave. I think he still loves *you* and has been leading this poor lass astray."

"What do you like for breakfast?" Hannah asked Bech, as wearily as if she and not he had been awake all night. Himself, he felt oddly fit, for being fifty and on

the underside of the world. "Tell me about Afghanistan
—should I go there?" he said to Moira, and he settled
beside her on the carpeted divan while Hannah, in her
lumpy blue robe, shuffled in the kitchen, making his
breakfast. "Grapefruit if you have it," he shouted to her,
interrupting the start of Moira's word tour of Kabul.
"Otherwise, orange juice." *My God*, he thought to himself, *she has become my wife. Already I'm flirting with
another woman.*

Bech boarded the plane (from Australia, from Canada)
so light-headed with lack of sleep it alarmed him hardly
at all when the machine rose into the air. His stomach
hurt as if lined with grit, his face looked gray in the
lavatory mirror. His adventures seemed perilous, viewed
backward. Mysterious diseases, strange men laughing in
the night, loose women. He considered the nation he was
returning to: its riots and scandals, its sins and power and
gnashing metal. He thought of Bea, his plump suburban
softy, her belly striated with fine silver lines, and vowed
to marry her, to be safe.

The Holy Land

I *never should have married a Christian*, Bech thought, fighting his way up the Via Dolorosa. His bride of some few months, Beatrice Latchett (formerly Cook) Bech, and the Jesuit archaeologist that our Jewish-American author's hosts at the Mishkenot Sha'ananim had provided as guide to the Christian holy sites—a courtly Virgil to Bech's disbelieving Dante—kept getting ahead of him, their two heads, one blond and one bald, piously murmuring together as Bech fell behind in the dusty jostle of nuns and Arab boys, of obese Protestant pilgrims made bulkier still by airline tote bags. The incessant procession was watched by bored gaunt merchants with three-day beards as they stood before their souvenir shops. Their dark accusing sorrow plucked at Bech. His artist's eye, always, was drawn to the irrelevant: the overlay of commercialism upon this ancient sacred way fascinated him— Kodachrome where Christ stumbled, bottled Fanta where He thirsted. Scarves, caftans, olive-wood knickknacks begged to be bought. As a child, Bech had worried that merchants would starve; Union Avenue in Williamsburg, near where his uncles lived on South Second Street, had been lined with disregarded narrow shops, a Kafka world of hunger artists waiting unwatched in their cages. This was worse.

Père Gibergue had confirmed what Bea already knew from her guidebooks: the route Jesus took from Pilate's verdict to Golgotha was highly problematical, and in any case, all the streets of first-century Jerusalem were buried under twelve feet of rubble and subsequent paving. So they and their fellow pilgrims were in effect treading on air. The priest, wearing flared slacks and a short-sleeved shirt, stopped to let Bech catch up, and pointed out to him overhead a half-arch dating, it seemed certain, from the time of Herod. The other half of the arch was buried, lost, behind a gray façade painted with a polyglot array in which Bech could read the word GIFTS. Bea's face, beside the tanned face of the archaeologist, looked radiantly pale. She was lightly sweating. Her guidebook was clutched to her blouse like a missal. "Isn't it all wonderful?" she asked her husband.

Bech said, "I never realized what a big shot Herod was. I thought he was just something on the back of a Christmas card."

Père Gibergue, in his nearly flawless English, pronounced solemnly, "He was a crazy man, but a great builder." There was something unhappy about the priest's nostrils, Bech thought; otherwise, his vocation fit him like a smooth silk glove.

"There were several Herods," Bea interposed. "Herod

the Great was the slaughter-of-the-innocents man. His son Herod Antipas was ruling when Jesus was crucified."

"Wherever we dig now, we find Herod," Père Gibergue said, and Bech thought, *Science has seduced this man. In his archaeological passion, he has made a hero of a godless tyrant.* Jerusalem struck Bech as the civic embodiment of conflicted loyalties. At first, deplaning with Bea and being driven at night from the airport to the Holy City through occupied territory, he had been struck by the darkness of the land, an intended wartime dark such as he had not seen since his GI days, in the tense country nightscapes of England and Normandy. Their escort, the son of American Zionists who had emigrated in the Thirties, spoke of the convoys that had been forced along this highway in the '67 war, and pointed out some hilly places where the Jordanian fire had been especially deadly. Wrecked tanks and trucks, unseeable in the dark, had been left as monuments. Bech remembered, as their car sped vulnerably between the black shoulders of land, the sensation (which for him had been centered in the face, the mouth more than the eyes—had he been more afraid of losing his teeth than his sight?) of being open to bullets, which there was no dodging. Before your brain could register anything, the damage would be done. Teeth shattered, the tongue torn loose, blood gushing through the punctured palate.

Then, as the car entered realms of light—the suburbs of Jerusalem—Bech was reminded of southern California, where he had once gone on a fruitless flirtation with some movie producers, who had been unable to wrap around his old novel *Travel Light* a package the banks would buy. Here were the same low houses and palm fronds, the same impression of staged lighting, exclusively frontal, as if the backs of these buildings dissolved into unpainted slats and rotting canvas, into weeds and warm air—that stagnant, balmy, expectant air of Hollywood when the sun goes down. The Mishkenot—the official city guesthouse, where this promising fifty-two-year-old writer and his plump Protestant wife were to stay for three weeks—seemed solidly built of the same stuff of cinematic illusion: Jerusalem limestone, artfully pitted by the mason's chisel, echoing like the plasterboard corridors of a Cecil B. De Mille temple to the ritual noises of weary guests unpacking. A curved staircase of mock-Biblical masonry led up to an alcove where a desk, a map, a wastebasket, and a sofa awaited his meditations. Bech danced up and down these stairs with an enchantment born in cavernous movie palaces; he was Bojangles, he was Astaire, he was George Sanders, wearing an absurd headdress and a sneer, exulting in the captivity and impending torture of a white-limbed maiden who, though so frightened her jewels chatter, will not forswear her Jahweh. Israel had no other sentimental significance for him; his father, a Marxist of a theoretical and unenrolled sort, had lumped the Zionists with all the *Luftmenschen* who imagined that mollifying exceptions might be stitched into the world's cruel and necessary patchwork of rapine and exploitation. To postwar Bech, busy in Manhattan, events in Palestine had passed as one more mop-up scuffle, though involving a team with whom he identified as effortlessly as with the Yankees.

Bea, an Episcopalian, was enraptured simply at being on Israel's soil. She kept calling it "the Holy Land." In the morning, she woke him to share what she saw: through leaded windows, the Mount of Olives, tawny and cypress-strewn, and the silver bulbs of a Russian church gleaming in the Garden of Gethsemane. "I never thought I'd be here, *ever*," she told him, and as she turned, her face seemed still to brim with reflected morning light. Bech kissed her and over her shoulder read a multilingual warning not to leave valuables on the window sill.

"Why didn't you ask Rodney to bring you," he asked, "if it meant so much?"

"Oh, Rodney. His idea of a spiritual adventure was to go backpacking in Maine."

Bech had married this woman in a civil ceremony in lower Manhattan on an April afternoon of unseasonable chill and spitting snow. She was the younger, gentler sister of a mistress he had known for years and with whom he had always fought. He and Bea rarely fought, and at his age this appeared possibly propitious. He had married her to escape his famous former self. He had given up his apartment at Ninety-ninth and Riverside— an address consecrated by twenty years of *Who's Who*s —to live with Bea in Ossining, with her twin girls and only son. These abrupt truths raced through his mind, marvellously strange, as he contemplated the radiant stranger whom the world called his wife. "Why didn't you tell me," he asked her now, "you took this kind of thing so much to heart?"

"You knew I went to church."

"The E*pis*copal church. I thought it was a social obligation. Rodney wanted the kids brought up in the upper middle class."

"He thought that would happen anyway. Just by their being his children."

"Lord, I don't know if I can hack this: be an adequate stepfather to the kids of a snob and a Christian fanatic."

"Henry, this is your Holy Land, too. You should be thrilled to be here."

"It makes me nervous. It reminds me of *Samson and Delilah.*"

"You *are* thrilled. I can tell." Her blue eyes, normally as pale as the sky when the milkiest wisps of strato-cirrus declare a storm coming tomorrow, looked up at him with a new, faintly forced luster. The Holy Land glow. Bech found it distrustworthy, yet, by some twist, in some rarely illumined depth of himself, flattering. While he was decoding the expression of her eyes, her mouth was forming words he now heard, on instant replay, as "Do you want to make love?"

"Because we're in the Holy Land?"

"I'm so excited," Bea confessed. She blushed, waiting. Another hunger artist.

"This is blasphemous," Bech protested. "Anyway, we're being picked up to sight-see in twenty minutes. What about breakfast instead?" He kissed her again, feeling estranged. He was too old to be on a honeymoon. His marriage was like this Zionist state they were in: a mistake long deferred, a miscarriage of passé fervor and antiquated tribal righteousness, an attempt to be safe on an earth where there was no safety.

Their quarters in the Mishkenot included a kitchen. Bea called from within it, "There's two sets of silver. One says Dairy and the other says Meat."

"Use one or the other," Bech called back. "Don't mingle them."

"What'll happen if I do?"

"I don't know. Try it. Maybe it'll trip the trigger and bring the Messiah."

"Now who's being blasphemous? Anyway, the Messiah *did* come."

"We can't all read His calling card."

Her only answer was the clash of silver.

I'm too old to be married, Bech thought, though he smiled to himself as he thought it. He went to the window and looked at the view that had sexually stimulated his wife. Beyond the near, New Testament hills the color of unglazed Mexican pottery were lavender desert mountains like long folds in God's lap.

"Is there anything I should know about eggs and butter?" Bea called.

"Keep them away from bacon."

"There isn't any bacon. There isn't any meat in the fridge at all."

"They didn't trust you. They knew you'd try to do something crummy." His Christian wife was thirteen years younger than he. Her belly bore silver stretch marks from carrying twins. She made gentle yipping noises when she fucked. Bech wondered whether he had ever really been a sexy man, or was it just an idea that went with bachelorhood? He had been a satisfactory sprinter, he reflected, but nobody up to now had challenged his distance capacity. At his age, he should be jogging.

The first sight they were taken to, by a Jewish archaeologist in rimless glasses, was the Wailing Wall. It was a Saturday. Sabbath congregations were gathered in the sun of the limestone plaza the Israelis had created by bulldozing away dozens of Arab homes. People were chanting, dancing; photographs were forbidden. Men in sidelocks were leaning their heads against the wall in prayer, the broad-brimmed hats of the Hasidim tipped askew. The archaeologist told Bech and Bea that for a millennium the wall could not be seen from where they stood, and pointed out where the massive, characteristically edged Herodian stones gave way to the smaller stones of Saladin and the Mamelukes. Bea urged Bech to walk up to the wall. The broad area in front of it had been designated a synagogue, with separate male and female sections, so they could not pass in through the fence together. "I won't go where you can't go," he said.

Bech's grandfather, a diamond-cutter and disciple of Spinoza, had come to the United States from the ghetto of Amsterdam in 1880; Bech's father had been an atheistic socialist; and in Bech socialist piety had dwindled to a stubborn wisp of artistic conscience. So there was little in his background to answer to the unearthly ardor of Bea's urging. "I want you to, Henry. Please."

He said, "I don't have a hat. You have to have a hat."

"They have paper yarmulkes there. In that basket," the archaeologist offered, pointing. He was a short bored bearded man, whose attitude expressed no wish, himself, to approach the wall. He stood on the blinding limestone of the plaza as if glued there by his shadow.

"Let's skip it," Bech said. "I get the idea from here."

"No, Henry," Bea said. "You must go up and touch it. You must. For me. Think. We may never be here again."

In her plea he found most touching the pronoun "we." Ever since his honorable discharge from the armed forces, Bech had been an I. He picked a black paper hat from the basket, and the hat was unwilling to adhere to his head; his hair was too woolly, too fashionably full-bodied. Graying had made it frizzier. A little breeze seemed to be blowing outward from the wall and twice threatened to lift his yarmulke away. Amid the stares of congregated Hasidic youth, their side curls as menacing as lions' manes, he held the cap to the back of his skull with his hand and approached, step by cautious step, all that remained of the Temple.

It was, the wall, a Presence. The great rectangular Herodian stones, each given a shallow border, like a calling card, by the ancient masons, were riddled with lice. Into the cracks of erosion, tightly folded prayers had been stuffed—the more he looked, the more there were. Bech supposed paper lasted forever in this Californian climate. The space around him, the very air, felt tense, like held breath. Numbly he reached out, and as he touched the surprisingly warm sacred surface, an American voice whined into his ears from a small circle of

Hasidim seated on chairs nearby. "Who is this God?" the voice was asking loudly. "If He's so good, why does He permit all the pain in the world? Look at Cambodia, man. . . ." The speaker and his audience were undergoing the obligatory exercise of religious debate. The Jewish tongue, divinely appointed to be active. Bech closed his ears and backed away rapidly. The breeze made another grab at his paper yarmulke. He dropped the flimsy thing into the basket, and Bea was waiting on the other side of the fence.

She was beaming, proud; he had been attracted to that in her which so purely encouraged him. Amid many in this last, stalled decade of his who had wished to reshape, to activate him forcefully, she had implied that his perfection lay nowhere but in a deepening of the qualities he already possessed. Since he was Jewish, the more Jewish he became in her Christian care, the better.

"Wasn't it wonderful?" she asked.

"It was something," was all he would grant her. Strange diseases, he thought, demand strange remedies: he, her. As they linked arms, after the separation imposed by a sexist orthodoxy, Bech apprehended Bea with refreshed clarity, by this bright, dry light of Israel: as a creature thickening in the middle, the female of a species mostly hairless and with awkward gait, her flesh nearing the end of its reproductive capacity and her brain possessed by a bizarre creed, yet pleasing to him and asking for his loyalty as unquestioningly, as helplessly as she gave him hers.

Their guide led them up a slanted road, past an adolescent soldier with a machine gun, to the top of the wall.

On their left, the faithful continued to circle and pray; on their right, a great falling off disclosed the ugly results of archaeology, a rubble of foundations. "The City of David," their guide said proudly, "just where the Bible said it would be. Everything," he said, and his gesture seemed to include all of the Holy City, "just as it was written. We read first, then we dig." At the Gate of the Moors, their guide yielded to a courtly Arab professor— yellow face, brown suit, Oxford accent—who led them in stockinged feet through the two mosques built on the vast platform that before 70 A.D. had supported the Temple. Strict Jewish believers never came here, for fear of accidentally treading upon the site of the Holy of Holies, the Ark of the Covenant. Within the Aqsa Mosque, Bech and Bea were informed of recent violence: King Abdullah of Jordan had been assassinated near the entrance in 1951, before the eyes of his grandson the present King Hussein; and in 1969, a crazed Australian had attempted to set the end nearest Mecca afire, with considerable success. Craziness, down through history, has performed impressively, Bech thought.

They were led past a scintillating fountain, up a few marble stairs, to the Dome of the Rock. Inside an octagon of Persian tile, beneath a dizzyingly lavish and symmetrical upward abyss, a spine of rock, the tip of Mount Moriah, showed where Abraham had attempted to sacrifice Isaac and, failing that, had founded three religions. Here also, the professor murmured amid the jostle of the faithful and the touring, Cain and Abel had made their fatally contrasting offerings, and Mohammed had ascended to Heaven on his remarkable horse Burak, whose hoofprints the pious claim to recognize, along with the fingerprints of an angel who restrained the Rock from going to Heaven also. For reasons known best to themselves, the Crusaders had hacked at the Rock. Great hackers, the Crusaders. And Suleiman the Magnificent, who had wrested the Rock back from the (from his standpoint) infidels, had his name set in gold on high, within the marvellous dome. The King of Morocco had donated the green carpets, into which Bea's stockinged feet dug impatiently, aching to move on from these empty wonders to the Christian sites. *Sexy little feet*, Bech thought; from his earliest amours, he had responded to the dark band of reinforcement that covers half of a woman's stockinged toes, giving us eight baby cleavages.

"Do you wish to view the hairs from the Beard of the Prophet?" the professor asked, adding, "There is always a great crowd around them."

Hairs of the Prophet were the kind of sight Bech liked, but he said, "I think my wife wants to push on."

They were led down from Herod's temple platform along a peaceable path beside an Arab cemetery. Their guide suddenly chuckled; his teeth were as yellow as his face. He gestured at a bricked-up portal in the Old City wall. "That is the Golden Gate, the gate whereby the Messiah is supposed to come, so the Ommiads walled it solid and, furthermore, put a cemetery there, because the Messiah supposedly is unable to walk across the dead."

"Hard to go anywhere if that's the rule," Bech said, glancing sideways to see how Bea was bearing up under

: 77 :

these malevolent overlays of superstition. She looked pink, damp, and happy, her Holy Land glow undimmed. At the end of the pleasant path, at the Lion's Gate, they were passed into the care of the debonair Jesuit and embarked upon the Via Dolorosa.

Lord, don't let me suffocate, Bech thought. The priest kept leading them underground, to show them buried Herodian pools, Roman guardrooms that the sinkage of centuries had turned into grottoes, and paving stones scratched by the soldiers as they played the game of kings—proof, somehow, of the historical Jesus. Père Gibergue knew his way around. He darted into the back room of a bakery, where a dirty pillar of intense archaeological interest stood surrounded by shattered crates. By another detour, Bech and Bea were led onto the roof of the Church of the Holy Sepulcher; here an ancient company of Abyssinian monks maintained an African village of rounded huts and sat smiling in the sun. One of them posed for Bea's camera standing against a cupola. Below the cupola, Père Gibergue explained with archaeological zeal, was the crypt where Saint Helena, mother of Constantine, discovered in the year 327 the unrotted wood of the True Cross. To their guide's sorrow, the young Russian Orthodox priest (his face waxen-white, his thin beard tapered to a double point: the very image, as Bech imagined it, of Ivan Karamazov) who answered their ring at the door of the Alexandra Hostel refused to admit them, this being a Sabbath, to the excavated cellar wherein had been found a worn threshold certainly stepped upon by the foot of God Incarnate.

So this is what's been making the goyim tick all these years. All these levels—roofs coterminous with the street, sacred footsteps buried meters beneath their own—afflicted Bech like a sea of typographical errors. Perhaps this was life: mistake heaped upon mistake, one protein molecule entangled with another until the confusion thrived. Except that it smelled so fearfully dead. The Church of the Holy Sepulcher was so needlessly ugly that Bech said to Bea, "You should have let the Arabs design it for you."

Père Gibergue overheard and said, "In fact, an Arab family has been entrusted with the keys for eight hundred years, to circumvent the contention among the Christian sects." Inside the hideous edifice, the priest, too, seemed overwhelmed; he sat on a bench near some rusting pipe scaffolding and said, "Go. I will pray here while you look." He hid his face in his hands.

Undaunted, Bea with her guidebook led Bech up a marble staircase to the site of the Crucifixion. This turned out to be a great smoke-besmirched heap or fungus of accreted icons and votive lamps. Six feet from the gold-rimmed hole where Christ's cross had supposedly been socketed, a fat Greek priest, seated in his black muffin hat at a table peddling candles, was taking a swig from a bottle in a paper bag. At Bech's side, Bea did a genuflective dip and gazed enthralled at this mass of aesthetic horrors. German tourists were noisily shuffling about, exploding flashbulbs.

"Let's go," Bech muttered.

"Oh, Henry, why?"

"This frightens me." It had that alchemic stink of medieval basements where vapors condensed as demons and pogroms and autos-da-fé. Torquemada, Hitler, the czars—every despot major or minor who had tried to stunt and crush his race had inhaled these Christly vapors. He dragged Bea away, back down to the main floor of the church, which her guidebook itself admitted to be a *conglomeration of large and small rooms, impossible to consider as a whole.*

Père Gibergue unbowed the tan oval of his head. He asked hopefully, "Enough?"

"More than," Bech said.

The Jesuit nodded. "A great pity. This should be Chartres. Instead . . ." He told Bea, "With your camera, you should photograph that, what the Greeks are doing. Without anyone's permission, they are walling up their sector of the nave. It is barbarous. But not untypical."

Bea peered through a gilded grate into a sector of holy space crowded with scaffolding and raw pink stone. She did not lift her camera. She had been transported, Bech realized, to a realm beyond distaste. "We cannot go without visiting the Sepulcher of Christ," she announced.

Père Gibergue said, "I advise against it. The line is always long. There is nothing to see. Believe me."

Bech echoed, "Believe him."

Bea said, "I don't expect to be here ever again," and got into line to enter a little building that reminded Bech, who joined her, of nothing so much as those mysteriously ornate structures that used to stand in discreet corners of parks in Brooklyn and the Bronx, too grand for lawn mowers but unidentified as latrines; he had always wondered what had existed inside such dignified small buildings—mansions in his imagination for dwarfs. The line moved slowly, and the faces of those returning looked stricken.

There were two chambers. The outer held a case containing a bit of the stone that the Angel is said to have rolled away from the mouth of the tomb; a German woman ahead of Bech in line kissed the cracked glass top of the case and caressed herself in an elaborate spasm of pious gratification, eyeballs rolling, a dovelike moan bubbling from her throat. He was relieved that Bea was better behaved: she glanced down, made a mental note, and passed by. He gazed upon the whitish hair pinned up above the damp nape of her neck as if seeing it for the last time. They were about to be separated by an infamous miracle.

The inner chamber was entered by an opening so small Bech had to crouch, though the author was not tall. Within, as had been foretold, there was "nothing to see." Smoking lamps hanging thick as bats from the low ceiling. A bleak marble slab. No trace of the original sepulcher hewn from the rock of Golgotha. In the confines of this tiny space, elbow to elbow with Bech, another stocky Greek priest, looking dazed, was waving lighted tapers held cleverly between his spread fingers. The tapers were for sale. The priest looked at Bech. Bech didn't buy. With a soft grunt of irritation, the priest waved the lighted tapers out. Bech was fascinated by this sad moment of disappointed commerce; he imagined how the wax must drip onto the man's fat fingers, how it must sting. A hunger artist. The priest eyed Bech again. The whites above his dolefully sagging lower lids were very bloodshot. Smoke gets in your eyes.

Back in their room at the Mishkenot, he asked Bea, "How's your faith?"

"Fine. How's yours?"

"I don't know much about places of worship, but wasn't that the most God-forsaken church you ever did see?"

"It's history, Henry. You have to see through external accidents to the things of the spirit. You weren't religiously and archaeologically prepared. The guidebook warns people they may be disappointed."

"Disappointed! Disgusted. Even your poor Jesuit, who's been there a thousand times, had to hide his face in his hands. Did you hear him complain about what the Greeks were doing to their slice of the pie? Did you hear his story about the Copts swooping down one night and slapping up a chapel that then couldn't be taken away for some idiotic superstitious reason?"

"They wanted to be close to the Holy Sepulcher," Bea said, stepping out of her skirt.

"I've never seen anything like it," Bech said. "It was garbage, of an ultimate sort."

"It was beautiful to be there, just beautiful," Bea said, skinning out of her blouse and bra in one motion.

How, Bech asked himself, out of a great materialist

nation containing one hundred million fallen-away Christians had he managed to pick this one radiant aberrant as a bride? *Instinct*, he answered himself; his infallible instinct for the distracting. At the height of the lovemaking that the newlyweds squeezed into a shadowy hour before they were due to go out to dinner, the bloodshot eyeball of the unsuccessful taper-selling priest returned to him, sliding toward Bech as toward a demon brother unexpectedly encountered while robbing the same tomb.

The dinner was with Israeli writers, in a restaurant staffed by Arabs. Arabs, Bech perceived, are the blacks of Israel. Slim young men, they came and went silently, accepting orders and serving while the lively, genial, grizzled, muscular intellectuals talked. The men were an Israeli poet, a novelist, and a professor of English; their wives were also a poet, a novelist, and a professor, though not in matching order. All six had immigrated years ago and therefore were veterans of several wars; Bech knew them by type, fell in with their warmth and chaffing as if back into a party of uncles and cousins. Yet he scented something outdoorsy, an unfamiliar toughness, a readiness to fight that he associated with Gentiles, as part of the psychic kit that included their indiscriminate diet and their bloody, lurid religion. And these Jews had the uneasiness, the slight edge, of those with something to hold on to. The strength of the Wandering Jew had been that, at home nowhere specific, he had been at home in the world. The poet, a man whose face appeared incessantly to smile, broadened as it was by prominent ears and a concentration of wiry hair above the ears, said of the Wailing Wall, "The stones seem smaller now. They looked bigger when you could see them only up close."

The professor's wife, a novelist, took fire: "What a reactionary thing to say! I think it is beautiful, what they have done at the Kotel Ha. They have made a sacred space of a slum."

Bech asked, "There were many Arab homes?"

The poet grimaced, while the shape of his face still smiled. "The people were relocated, and compensated."

The female novelist told Bech, "Before '67, when the Old City was theirs, the Jordanians built a hotel upon the Mount of Olives, using the old tombstones for the soldiers' barracks. It was a vast desecration which they committed in full view. We felt very frustrated."

The male novelist, whose slender, shy wife was a poetess, offered as a kind of truce, "And yet I feel at peace in the Arab landscape. I do not feel at peace in Tel Aviv, among those Miami Beach hotels. That was not the idea of Israel, to make another Miami Beach."

"What was the idea, then?" asked the female novelist, teasing—an overweight but still-dynamic flirt among hirsute reactionaries. There is a lag, Bech thought, between the fading of an attractive woman's conception of herself and the fading of the reality.

The male novelist, his tanned skin minutely veined and ponderously loose upon his bones, turned to Bech with a gravity that hushed the table; an Arab waiter, ready to serve, stood there frozen. "The idea," it was stated to

Bech in the halting murmur of an extreme confidence, "is not easy to express. Not Freud and Einstein, but not Auschwitz, either. Something . . . in between."

Bech's eye flicked uneasily to the waiter and noticed the name on his identification badge: SULEIMAN.

The poetess, as if to lighten her husband's words, asked the American guests, "What have been your impressions so far? I know the question is foolish, you have been here a day."

"A day or a week," the female novelist boisterously volunteered, "Henry Bech will go back and write a best-selling book about us. Everyone does."

The waiter began to serve the food—ample, de-racinated, Hilton food—and while Bech was framing a politic answer, Bea spoke up for him. He was as startled as if one of his ribs had suddenly chirped. "Henry's in raptures," she said, "and so am I. I can't believe I'm here, it's like a dream."

"A costly dream," said the professor, the youngest of the men and the only one wearing a beard. "A dream costly to many men." His beard was as red as a Viking's; he stroked it a bit preeningly.

"The Holy Land," Bea went on, undeterred, her voice flowing like milk poured from above. "I feel I was born here. Even the air is so *right*."

Her strangeness, to her husband at this moment, did verge on the miraculous. At this table of Jews who, wearied of waiting for the Messiah, had altered the world on their own, Bea's voice with its lilt of hasty good news came as an amazing interruption. Bech answered the poetess as if he had not been interrupted. "It reminds me of southern California. The one time I was there, I felt surrounded by enemies. Not people like you," he diplomatically amended, "but up in the hills. Sharpshooters. Agents."

"You were there before Six-Day War," joked the female professor; until then, she had spoken not a word, merely smiled toward her husband, the smiling poet. It occurred to Bech that perhaps her English was insecure, that these people were under no obligation to know English, that on their ground it was his obligation to speak Hebrew. English, that bastard child of Norman knights and Saxon peasant girls—how had he become wedded to it? There was something diffuse and eclectic about the language that gave him trouble. It ran against his grain; he tended to open books and magazines at the back and read the last pages first.

"What shall we do?" the flamboyant female novelist was urgently asking him, evidently apropos of the state of Israel. "We can scarcely speak of it anymore, we are so weary. We are weary of war, and now we are weary of talk of peace."

"The tricky thing about peace," Bech suggested, "is that it doesn't always come from being peaceable."

She laughed, sharply, a woman's challenging laugh. "So you, too, are a reactionary. Myself, I would give them anything—the Sinai, the West Bank. I would even give them back East Jerusalem, to have peace."

"*Not* East Jerusalem!" the Christian in their midst exclaimed. "Jerusalem," Bea said, "belongs to everybody."

And her face, aglow with confidence in things unseen,

became a cause for wonder among the seven others. The slim, shy poetess, whose half-gray hair was parted in the exact center of her slender skull, asked lightly, "You would like to live here?"

"We'd love to," Bea said.

Bech felt he had to step on this creeping "we" of hers. "My wife speaks for herself," he said. "Her enthusiasm overwhelmed even the priest who took us up the Via Dolorosa this afternoon. My own impression was that the Christian holy sites are hideously botched. I liked the mosques."

Bea explained with the patience of a saint, "I said to myself, I've waited for this for thirty-nine years, and I'm not going to let anybody, even my husband, ruin it for me."

Sunday-school pamphlets, Bech imagined. Bible illustrations protected by a page of tissue paper. Bea had carried those stylized ochre-and-moss-green images up from infancy and, when the moment had at last arrived, had placed them carefully upon the tragic, eroded hills of Jerusalem and pronounced the fit perfect. He loved her for that, for remaining true to the little girl she was. In the lull of silence her pious joy had induced, Suleiman came and offered them dessert, which the sated Israelis refused. Bech had apple pie, Bea had fig sherbet, to the admiration of their hosts. Young in marriage, young in appetite.

"You know," he told her in the taxi back to the Mishkenot, "the Holy Land isn't holy to those people tonight the way it is to you."

"I know that, of course."

"To them," he felt obliged to press on, "it's holy because it *is* land at all; after nineteen hundred years of being pushed around, the Jews have a place where they can say, O.K., this is it, this is our country. I don't think it's something a Christian can understand."

"I certainly can. Henry, it saddens me that you feel you must explain all this to me. Rodney and I once went to a discussion group on Zionism. Ask me about Herzl. Ask me about the British Mandate."

"I explain it only because you've surprised me with your own beliefs."

"I'll keep them to myself if they embarrass you."

"No, just don't offer to immigrate. They don't want you. Me, they wouldn't mind, but I have enough problems right now."

"I'm a problem."

"I didn't say that. My work is a problem."

"I think you'd work very well here."

"Jesus, no. It's depressing. To me, it's just a ghetto with farms. I *know* these people. I've spent my whole life trying to get away from them, trying to think bigger."

"Maybe that's your problem. Why try to get away from being Jewish? All those motorcycles, and Cincinnati, and Saint Bernard—you have to make it all up. Here, it'd be real for you. You could write and I could join a dig, under Father Gibergue."

"What about your children?"

"Aren't there kibbutz schools?"

"For Episcopalians?"

She began to cry, out of a kind of sweet excess, as

when angels weep. "I thought you'd like it that I love it here," she got out, adding, "with you."

"I *do* like it. Don't you like it that I like it in Ossining, with you?" As their words approached nonsense, some dim sense of what the words "holy land" might mean dawned on him. The holy land was where you accepted being. Middle age was a holy land. Marriage.

Back in their room in the Mishkenot, a calling card had been left on a brass tray. Bech looked at the Hebrew lettering and said, "I can't read this."

"I can," Bea said, and turned the card over, to the Roman type on the other side.

"What does it say?"

Bea palmed the card and looked saucy. "My secret," she said.

I never should have married a Christian, Bech told himself, without believing it. He was smiling at the apparition of his plump Wasp wife, holding a calling card shaped like a stone in Herod's wall.

Wifely, she took pity. "Actually, it's somebody from *The Jerusalem Post*. Probably wanting an interview."

"Oh God," Bech said.

"I suppose he'll come again," Bea offered.

"Let's hope not," Bech said, blasphemously.

Macbech

Bea on her mother's side was a Sinclair, and a long-held dream of hers had been to visit the land of her ancestors—the counties of Sutherland and Caithness in the eastern Scots Highlands. Bech, now legally established in the business of making her dreams come true, and slightly enriched by the sale of a forgotten *Collier's* chestnut to a public-television series promoting Minor Masters of the American Short Story, volunteered to take her there, as a fortieth-birthday present. They parked their crumbling mock-Tudor manse in Ossining and its three juvenile inhabitants with a house-sitting young faculty couple from Mercy College and flew that May to London, entraining north to Edinburgh and thence to Inverness. Bech liked Great Britain, since its decline was as notorious as his, and he liked trains, for the same reason. The farther north they went, the strangely happier he became.

His happiness first hit him in Edinburgh, as he lugged

their suitcases up a mountainous flight of stairs from the sunken glass-and-iron sheds of Waverley Station. As he turned onto North Bridge, at the far end of which their hotel waited, his eyes confronted not metropolitan rectangles but a sweeping green shoulder of high and empty land named, Bea read at his straining side from out of her blue guidebook, Arthur's Seat. Burdened by baggage as he was, Bech felt lifted up, into the airy and the epic. Scotland seemed at a glance ancient, raw, grimy, lush, mysterious, and mannerly. Like Bech it was built solid of disappointments. Lost causes abounded. Defenders of the Castle were promptly hanged outside the Portcullis Gate, witches were burned in bundles, Covenanters were slaughtered. In Holyrood Palace, the red-haired Queen of the Scots, taller than one had expected, slipped in her brocaded slippers down a spiral stone staircase to visit the handsome boy Darnley, who, devoid of all common sense, one evening burst into her little supper room and, with others, dragged off her pet secretary David Rizzio and left him in the audience chamber dead of fifty-six stab wounds. *The alleged indelible stain of blood, if it exists, is concealed by the floor covering. Jealousy of Rizzio's political influence, and perhaps a darker suspicion in Darnley's mind, were the probable motives for the crime.* Dried blood and dark suspicions dominated the Caledonian past; nothing sinks quicker in history, Bech thought, than people's actual motives, unless it be their sexual charm. In this serene, schizophrenic capital —divided by the verdant cleavage of a loch drained in 1816—he admired the biggest monument ever erected to an author, a spiky huge spire sheltering a statue of Sir

Walter Scott and his dog, and he glanced, along the slant-ing Royal Mile, down minuscule alleys in the like of which Boswell had caught and clipped his dear prosti-tutes. "Heaven," Bech kept telling Bea, who began to resent it.

But Bech's abrasive happiness grew as, a few days later, the windows of their next train gave on the gorse-blotched slopes of the Grampians, authentic mountains green and gray with heather and turf. In Inverness, they rented a little cherry-red car in which everything nor-mally on the right was on the left; groping for the gear-shift, Bech grabbed air, and, peering into the rearview mirror, saw nothing. Bea, frightened, kept reminding him that she was there, on his left, and that he was driving terribly close to that stone wall. "Do you want to drive?" he asked her. At her expected answer of "Oh, no," he experimentally steered the short distance to Loch Ness; there they stood among the bright-yellow bushes on the bank, hoping to see a monster. The water, dark even in the scudding moments of sunlight, was chopped into lit-tle wavelets each shadow of which might be a fin, or a gliding nostril. "It could be," Bech said. "Remember the coelacanth."

His fair wife touched his arm and shivered. "Such dark water."

"They say the peat, draining into it. Tiny black parti-cles suspended everywhere, so all these expensive cameras they lower down can't see a thing. There could be whales down there."

Bea nodded, still staring. "It's much bigger than any-body says."

Married peace, that elusive fauna swimming in the dark also, stole back upon them at the hotel, a many-gabled brick Guests beside the pretty river Ness. After dinner, in the prolonged northern light, they wandered across a bridge and came by chance upon a stadium where a show for tourists was in progress: Scots children in kilts performed traditional dances to the bagpipes' keening. The couple loved, when they travelled, all children, having none of their own. Their marriage would always be sterile; Bea had been willing, though nearing the end of her fourth decade, but Bech shied from paternity, with its overwhelming implication of commitment. He aspired to be no more than one of mankind's uncles, and his becoming at a blow stepfather to Bea's twin adolescent girls, Ann and Judy, and to little Donald (who had at first called him "Mr. Bech" and then "Uncle Henry"), was bliss and burden enough, in the guardianship line. His books and in his fallow years his travels were his children, and by bringing Bea along he gave her what he could of fresh ties to the earth. Some of the Scots performers were so small they could barely hop across the swords laid flat on the grass, and some were tugged back and forth in the ritual patterns by their older sisters. Watching the trite, earnest routines, Bea beside Bech acquired a tranced smile; tears had appeared in her blue eyes without cancelling the smile, an unsurprising combination in this climate where sun and shower and rainbow so swiftly alternated. In the sheltered bleachers where they sat they seemed the only tourists; the rest were mothers and fathers and uncles, with children's raincoats in their laps. As Bech and Bea returned to their hotel, the still-twilit sky, full of hastening clouds, added some drops of silver to the rippling river that looked utterly pure, though it was fed by the black loch.

Next day they dared drive left-handedly along the crowded coast road north, through Dingwall and Tain, Dornoch and Golspie. At Dunrobin Castle, a downpour forbade that they descend into the famous formal gardens; instead they wandered unattended through room after panelled room, past portraits and stag horns and framed photographs of turn-of-the-century weekends, the Duke of Sutherland and his stiff guests in white flannels, holding tennis rackets like snowshoes. *"Its name,"* Bech read to Bea from the guidebook, *"may mean 'Robin's Castle,' after Robert, the sixth Earl of Sutherland, whose wife was a daughter of the barbarous Alexander, Earl of Buchan, a younger son of King Robert II and known as 'The Wolf of Badenoch.'* Now there's history," he said. " 'The barbarous Alexander.' The third Duke of Sutherland," he went on, paraphrasing, "was the largest landowner in Western Europe. Almost the whole county of Sutherland, over a million acres. His father and grandfather were responsible for the Clearances. They pushed all these poor potato farmers out so they could graze sheep—the closest thing to genocide in Europe up to Hitler, unless you count the Armenians in Turkey."

"Well, don't blame me," Bea said. "I was just a Sinclair."

"It was a man called John Sinclair who brought the Cheviot sheep north into Caithness."

"My mother's branch left around 1750."

"The Highlanders were looked at the same way the Victorians saw the Africans—savage, lazy, in need of improvement. That's what they called it, kicking the people out and replacing them with sheep. Improvement."

"Oh look, Henry! Queen Victoria slept in this bed. And she left her little lace gloves."

The bed had gilded posts but looked hard and small. *Uneasy lies the head.* Bech told Bea, "You really don't want to face it, do you? The atrocities a castle like this is built on." He heard his father in him speaking, and closed his mouth abruptly.

Bea's broad maternal face was flustered, pink, and damp in the humidity as rain slashed at the leaded windows overlooking the North Sea. "Well I hadn't thought to face it *now*, just because I'm a little bit Scotch."

"Scots," he corrected.

"The Sinclairs didn't order the Clearances, they were victims like everybody else."

"They had a castle," Bech said darkly.

"Not since the seventeenth century," Bea said back.

"I want to see the Strath Naver," he insisted. "That's where the worst of the Clearances were."

Back in the car, they looked at the map. "We can do it," Bea said, her wifely composure restored. "Go up through Wick and then around John o'Groats and over through Thurso and then down along the Strath Naver to Lairg. Though there won't be much to see, just empty land."

"That's the point," Bech said. "They moved the poor crofters out and then burned their cottages. It was the women, mostly, who resisted. The sheriff's men got drunk and whacked them on the head with truncheons and kicked them in their breasts."

"It was a terrible, terrible thing," Bea said, gently outflanking him. Her face looked luminous as harsh rain drummed on the roof of their little red English Ford, where everything was reversed. Her country, his patriotism. Her birthday, his treat. How strange, Bech bothered to notice, that his happiness in Scotland should take the form of being mean to her.

The Sinclairs had farmed, and perhaps a few did still farm, these great treeless fields of Caithness whose emerald sweep came right to the edge of the perilous cliffs. The cliffs, and the freestanding towers the sea had created from a millennial merging of those eroded ravines called gills, were composed of striations of gray sandstones as regular as the pages of a book. Down on the shore, vast, slightly tilted flagstones seemed to commemorate a giant's footsteps into the sea, or to attest to the ruin of a prodigious library. No fence prevented a tourist or a cow from toppling off and hurtling down the sheer height composed of so many accreted, eroding layers; paths had been beaten raggedly parallel to the cliff edge, leading to cairns whose explanatory legend was obscured by lichen and to, in one spot, an unofficial dump, where newspapers and condensed-milk cans had been deposited upon the edge of the precipice but had not all fallen in. Gulls nested just underneath the lip of the turf and in crannies straight down the cliff face; their white bodies, wings extended in flight, speckled the windy steep spaces between the surface of the twinkling sea and the edge where Bech and Bea stood. The plunging perspectives made her giddy, and she shrieked when, teasing, he took a few steps forward and reached down as if to steal a gull egg. The mother gull tipped her head and peered up at him with an unimpressed pink eye. Bech backed away, breathless. For all his boyish bravado, his knees were trembling. Heights called to him. *Fall. Fly.*

The wind so fierce no trees spontaneously grew in this northernmost county of Britain was a bright May breeze today, setting a blush on Bea's cheeks and flaring Bech's nostrils with the scent of salt spray. The Vikings had come to this coast, leaving ruin behind, and flaxen-haired infants. The houses of the region were low, with roofs of thatch or slate, and squared slabs of the ubiquitous flagstone had been set upright and aligned into fences along field boundaries. But the primary feel of this land was of unbounded emptiness, half-tamed and sweet, with scarce a car moving along the A9 and not another walking man or woman to be seen this side of the green horizon, beyond which meadows gave way to brown moors where peat was dug in big black bricks out of long straight trenches, and the emptiness began in earnest. Every cemetery they stopped at had its Sinclairs; Bea was excited to be on ancestral territory, though less ecstatic than she had been in Israel. Bech had felt crowded there, and here, in the many-pocketed tweed jacket he had bought along Princes Street and the droop-brimmed plaid bog hat purchased just yesterday in Wick, he felt at home. "This is my kind of place," he told Bea from the cliff edge, his breath regained and his knees again steady.

"You're just paying me back," she said, "for liking the Holy Land so much."

"That was overdeveloped. This is just right. Thousand-acre zoning."

"You look ridiculous in that hat," she told him unkindly, uncharacteristically. The wind, perhaps, had whipped a shine into her eyes. "I'm not sure the jacket suits you, either."

"They feel great. 'Blow, winds, and crack your cheeks!' "

"They give you that troll look."

"What troll look?"

"That troll look that—"

He finished for her. "That Jews get in tweeds. Shit. I've really done it. I've married an anti-Semite."

"I wasn't going to say that at all." But she never did supply what she had been going to say, and it was not until they were snuggled in their bed on the musty third floor of the Thurso Arms that the monsters in the deep space between them stopped shifting. The little brick city fell away beneath the gauze curtains of their windows like a town in one of the drabber fairy tales. They made love dutifully, since they had been given a double bed. There was no doubt, Bea did resent his taking Scotland so readily—so greedily—into himself. The stones and grass of this place, its pinnacles and cobbles and weatherswept grays, its history of constant, though turbulently contested, loss in relation to the cushioned green land to the south . . . weren't the Scots one of the ten lost tribes of Israel? Like the Jews, the Celts had been pushed aside from the European mainstream yet not thrown quite free of it: permitted, rather, to witness closely its ruthless forward roar and to harbor in wry hearts and pinched lives a criticism that became—beyond Spinoza and Hume, Maxwell and Einstein—America. Or so it seemed while Bea slept and Bech lay awake relishing the sensation of being, on the northern edge of this so thoroughly annotated island, in a kind of magical margin, the sky still white though the time approached midnight. From beneath his window arose the unexpected sound of raucous teen-age horseplay, a hungry scuffling and hooting that further enriched his mystical, global sensations. For surely, if Bech's own narrow and narcissistic life was miracle enough to write about, an interlocked miracle was the existence, wherever you went on a map, of other people living other lives.

Except, it seemed, in the Highlands. Often where a place name sprouted on the dotted red line of the road, there seemed to be nothing, not even the ruined walls of a single house. Nothing was left of men but this name on the map, and the patches of brighter green where, over a century ago, potato patches had been fertilized. Otherwise, mile after mile of tummocky brown turf unrolled with no more than an occasional river or lake for punctuation, or one of those purple-green protuberances, neither mountain nor hill, for which the only name could be "ben." Bech and Bea had driven west from Thurso above the sea and turned south along the Strath Naver, scene of the most infamous of the Clearances. Atrocity leaves no trace on earth, Bech saw. Nature shrugs, and regroups. Perhaps in Poland there were stretches made vacant like this. There seemed no trace of man but the road itself, which was single-track, with widened spots at intervals where a car could pull over to let another pass. The game did not take long to learn: when two vehicles approached, the drivers accelerated to reach the farthest possible turnout short of collision. Bea maintained that that wasn't the way the game was played at all; rather, drivers courteously vied for the privilege of pulling over and letting the other driver pass with a wave of cheerful gratitude. "Do you want to drive?" he asked her.

"Yes," she answered, unexpectedly.

He stopped the car and stepped out. He inhaled the immaculate Highland air. Small white and pink flowers starred the violet reaches of moor. The clouds leaned in their hurry to get somewhere, losing whole clumps of themselves. There were no sheep. These, too, had been cleared away. As Bea drove along, her chin tipped up with the mental effort of not swerving right, he read to her about the Clearances. *"We have no country to fight for. You robbed us of our country and gave it to the sheep. Therefore, since you have preferred sheep to men, let sheep defend you!"* he read, a lump in his throat at the thought of an army of sheep. Jewish humor. "That's what they said to the recruiters when they tried to raise an army in the Highlands to help fight the Crimean War. The lairds were basically war chieftains, and after the Scots were beaten at Culloden and there was no more war, the crofters, who paid their rent mostly with military service, had nothing to offer. The lairds had moved to London and that nice part of Edinburgh we saw and needed money now, and the way to get money was to rent their lands to sheep farmers from the south."

"That's sad," Bea said absently, pulling into a patch of dirt on the left and accepting a grateful wave from the flaxen-haired driver of a rattling old lorry.

"Well, there's a kind of a beauty to it," Bech told her. "The Duke of Sutherland himself came up from London to see what was the matter, and one old guy stood up in the meeting and told him, *It is the opinion of this county that should the Czar of Russia take possession of Dunrobin Castle and of Stafford House next term we couldn't expect worse treatment at his hands than we have experienced in the hands of your family for the last fifty years.*" Bech chuckled; he thought of ancestors of his own, evading enlistment on the opposite side of that same war. His mother's people had come from Minsk. History, like geography, excited and frightened him with the enormousness of life beyond his dwindling own.

Bea blinked and asked, "Why are you so enthusiastic about all this?"

"You mean you aren't?"

"It's sad, Henry. You're not looking at the scenery."

"I am. It's magnificent. But misery must be seen as part of the picture."

"Part of *our* picture, you mean. That's what you're rubbing my nose in. You bring me here as a birthday present but then keep reminding me of all these battles and evictions and starvation and greed, as if it applies to *us*. All right. We're mortal. We're fallible. But that doesn't mean we're necessarily cruel, too." One of the leaning, hurrying clouds was darker than the others and suddenly it began to rain, to hail, with such ferocity that Bea whimpered and pulled the car to a halt in a wide spot. The white pellets danced upward from the red hood as if sprung from there and not the sky; the frown within the air was like what the blind must confront before the light winks out entirely. Then the air brightened; the hail ceased; and through the luminous mist of its ceasing a rainbow appeared above the shadows of a valley where a cultivated field formed a shelf of smooth verdure. They had come down from the remotest Highlands into an area where cultivation began, and telephone wires underlined the majesty of the sub-arctic sky. They both climbed out of the little car, to be nearer the rainbow, which, longer in one leg than the other, receded from them, becoming a kind of smile upon the purple-green brow of a ben. Bech luxuriated in the wild beauty all around and said, "Let's buy a castle and murder King Duncan and settle down. This is where we belong."

"We do *not*," Bea cried. "It's where *I* belong!" He was startled; fear must have shown on his face, for an anxious wifely guilt blurred hers as, close to tears, she still pressed her point: "That's so *typ*ical of you writers—you appropriate. My own poor little Scottishness has been taken from me; you're more of a Scot now than I am. I'll have nothing left eventually, and you'll move on to appropriate somebody else's something. Henry, this marriage was a horrible mistake."

But the sheer horror of what she was saying drove her, her blurred round face pink and white like that of a rabbit, into his arms. He held her, patting her back while her sobs moistened his tweed shoulder and the rainbow quite faded in the gorse-golden sun. She was still try-ing to explain herself, her outburst. "Ever since we got married—"

"Yes?" he encouraged, noting above her sunny head that the lower slopes of the mountain, for aeons stark moor, had been planted in regiments of fir trees to feed the paper mills of the south.

"—I've felt myself in your mind, being di*gest*ed, be-coming a *char*acter."

"You're a very real person," he reassured her, patting mechanically. "You're my Christian maiden." In defer-ence to the prickly spine of feminist feeling that she had grown beneath his hands, he quickly amended this to: "God's Christian maiden."

Bech Wed

T HE HOUSE IN OSSINING was a tall mock-Tudor with
an incongruous mansard roof, set on a domed lawn
against a fringe of woods on an acre and a half tucked
somewhere between the Taconic State and the Briarcliff-
Peekskill parkways. Its exterior timbers were painted the
shiny harsh green of park benches and its stucco had
been aged to a friable tan; the interior abounded in
drafty wasteful spaces—echoing entrance halls and im-
perious wide staircases and narrow windowless corridors
for vanished servants to scuttle along. Bea and Rodney
while their marriage thrived had fixed it up, scraping the
white and then, next layer down, the dusty-rose paint off
the newel posts and banisters until natural oak was
reached; they had replaced all the broken glass and frag-
mented putty in the little greenhouse that leaned against
the library, retiled the upstairs bathrooms, replastered the
backstair walls, and laid down a lilac hedge and a composition tennis court. As their marriage ran into difficul-

ties, the scraping stopped halfway up the left-hand banister and the tennis court was taken over by the neighborhood children and their honey-limbed baby-sitters. Now Bech was installed in the mansion like a hermit crab tossed into a birdhouse. The place was much too big; he couldn't get used to the staircases and the volumes of air they arrogantly commandeered, or the way the heat didn't pour knocking out of steam radiators from an infernal source concealed many stories below but instead seeped from thin pipes sneaking low around the baseboards, pipes kept warm by personalized monthly bills and portentous, wheezing visits from the local oil truck. In the cellar, you could see the oil tanks—two huge rust-brown things greasy to the touch. And here was the furnace, an old converted coal-burner in a crumbling overcoat of plastered asbestos, rumbling and muttering all through the night like a madman's brain. Bech had hardly ever visited a basement before; he had lived in the air, like mistletoe, like the hairy sloth, Manhattan subgenus. Though he had visited his sister in Cincinnati, and written his freshest fantasy, *Travel Light*, upon impressions gathered during avuncular visits there, he had never in his bones known before what America was made of: lonely outposts, log cabins chinked with mud and moss.

Insulation was a constant topic of conversation with the neighbors, and that first winter Bech dragged his uprooted crab tail back and forth to the building-supply center along Route 9 and hauled home in Bea's sticky-geared Volare station wagon great rolls of pink insulation backed by silver paper; with a hardening right hand he stapled this cumbersome, airy material between the studs of an unused and never plastered third-floor room, intended for servants or storage, and made himself, all lined in silver imprinted with the manufacturer's slogans, a kind of dream-image, a surreal distillation, of his cloistered forsaken apartment high above the windswept corner of Ninety-ninth and Riverside. Here, his shins baking in the intersecting rays of two electric heaters, he was supposed to write.

"Write?" he said to Bea, who had proposed this space allocation. "How do you do that?"

"You know," she said, not to be joshed. "It'll all come back to you, now that you're settled and loved."

His heart, which had winced at "settled," fled from the word "loved" so swiftly that he went momentarily deaf. These happy conditions had nothing to do with writing. Happiness was not the ally but the enemy of truth. Dear Bea, standing there in her slightly shapeless housedress, her fair hair straggled out in the dishevelment of utter sincerity, seemed a solid obstacle to the translucent onrunning of the unease that was Bech's spiritual element, his punctilious modernist diet. Too complacent in her seventh-hand certainty, descended from Freud, that she held between her soft thighs the answer to all his questions, Bea assumed that the long sterile stretch of his unwed life before her had been, simply, a mistake, a wandering in a stony wilderness cluttered with women and trips. He doubted it was that simple. Being an artist was a matter of delicate and prolonged maneuver; who could tell where a false move lay? Think of Proust's, think of Rilke's, decades of procrastination. The derangement of the senses, Rimbaud had prescribed. Didn't all of Hart Crane's debauchery find its reason in a few incandescent lines that burned on long after the sullen waves had closed upon his suicide?

"What you must do," Bea told him, even as her blue Scots eyes slid sideways toward some other detail of housekeeping, "is go up there first thing every day and write a certain number of pages—not too many, or you'll scare yourself away. But do that number, Henry, good or bad, summer or winter, and see what happens."

"Good or bad?" he asked, incredulous.

"Sure, why not? Who can tell anyway, in the end? Look at Kafka, whom you admire so much. Who cares now, if *Amerika* isn't as good as *Das Schloss*? It's all Kafka, and that's all we care about. Whatever you produce, it'll be Bech, and that's all anybody wants out of you. *Mehr Licht; mehr Bech!*"

He hadn't known she knew all this German. "I don't admire Kafka," he grumbled, feeling a child's pleasurable restiveness. "I feel him as an oppressive older brother. He affects me the way his father affected him."

"What you're doing," Bea told him, "is punishing us. Ever since *The Chosen* got panned, you've been holding your breath like an angry baby. Enough now. Finish *Think Big*."

"I was thinking of calling it *Easy Money*."

"Good. A much better title. I think the old one intimidated you."

"But it's about New York. How can I write about New York when you've taken me away from it?"

"All the better," Bea briskly said, patting her hair in closer to the luminous orb of her face. "New York was a terrible place for you, you were always letting yourself get sidetracked."

"Who's to say," he asked, giving his old aesthetic one more try, "what a sidetrack is?"

"Simple. It's the one that doesn't lead anywhere. Do what you want with your talent. Hide it under a bushel. I can't stand here arguing forever. From the sounds out back, Donald and his friends are doing something terrible to the dog."

It was true, Donald and two pals from a house across the lane were trying to play rodeo with Max, a sluggish old golden retriever that Rodney and Bea had bought as a puppy. He had yelped when lassoed and then, as the boys were being scolded, hung his tail, ashamed of having tattled. Bech had never lived in close conjunction with a dog before. He marvelled at the range of emotion the animal could convey with its tail, its ears, and the flexible loose skin of its muzzle. When he and Bea returned from the supermarket or an expedition to the city, old Max in his simple-minded joy would flog the Volare fenders with his tail and, when his new master bent down to pat his head, would slip Bech's hand into his mouth and try to pull him toward the house—retrieving him, as it were. The grip of the dog's teeth, though kindly meant, was firm enough to give pain and to leave livid marks. Bech had to laugh, trying to pull his hand free without injury. Max's muzzle rumpled with fond determination as he kept tugging the stooping, wincing man toward the back door; his ears were rapturously flattened, and cats slid off the porch to rub at Bech's ankles jealously. Cats came with this house, and rodent pets of Donald's that died of escaping from their cages. The three children all had noisy friends, and Bea herself would spend many a morning and afternoon entertaining housewives from the neighborhood or from Briarcliff Manor or Pleasantville— old friends from the Rodney days, curious perhaps to glimpse the notorious author (in the suburbs, at least since *Peyton Place*, all authors are *sui generis* notorious) whom Bea—*Bea*, of all people—had somehow landed. If these visitors were there for morning coffee, they gave Bech little more than bright-eyed, wide-awake smiles above the crisp dickies stuck in their cashmere sweaters; but if he came upon them amid the lengthening shadows of the cocktail hour, slouched around second drinks in a murky corner of the timbered living room, these Gentile housewives would dart toward him blurred, expectant glances and, merriment waxing reckless, challenge him to "put" them "in" a book. Alas, what struck him about these women, in contrast to the women of his travels and of Manhattan, was just their undetachability from these, to him, illegible Westchester surroundings.

Without so many inducements to flee upstairs, Bech might never have settled into his silver room. But it was the one spot in the vast house where he did not seem to be in the middle of a tussle, or a party, or a concert. The twin girls especially could not bear to be out of range of amplified music. They were fifteen when Bech became their stepfather—rather bony, sallow girls with Rodney's broad forehead and solemn, slightly bulging gray eyes. They lolled on the sofa or upstairs in their room reading fat novels of witchcraft and horror in Maine while bathed in the clicking thud and apocalyptic lyrics of reggae. Donald, who had inherited more of Bea's curves and shades of humid pink, was ten, and for a time carried everywhere with him a battery-powered CB unit on which he attempted to chat with truckers rolling north beyond the woods. The sound of traffic, though kept at a distance, nevertheless permeated Westchester County, its pitch more sinister, because concealed by greenery, than the frank uproar of Manhattan. Marrying Bea, who had drifted into his life in the wake of her stormy sister, Bech had ignorantly climbed aboard an ark of suburban living whose engines now throbbed around him like those of a sinking merchant ship in Conrad. There was no ignoring noise in these environs. In New York, there were walls, precincts, zones and codes of avoidance; here in Ossining every disturbance had a personal application: the ringing phone was never in someone else's apartment, and the child crying downstairs was always one's own. A kind of siege crackled around the gawky half-green house, so conspicuous on its hillock of lawn—a siege of potentially disastrous groans in the plumbing and creaks in the woodwork, while the encircling animal world gnawed, fluttered, and scrabbled at the weakened structure. Invisible beetles and ants powdered the basement floor with their leavings, and Bech was astonished at how much infiltrating wildlife lurked in even a thoroughly tamed and mortgaged stretch of woods. Squirrels or was it bats danced over his head in the silver room, above the ceiling with its fantasy map of stains, within those dusty constructional gaps that merged with the teeming treetops via holes he could never spot from the ground or a ladder. Even in the summer he kept his room's one window closed against the distracting variety of birdcalls. That second spring a colorless small bird had built a nest in a chink of the eaves of the mansard roof and bewitched Bech with the incessancy of its trips to the nest. A fluffy beating of wings, an arousal of tiny cheeping, a momentary silencing of the cheeping with wriggling food, and then a beating of the wings away again. So much fanatic labor, to add a few mousy birds to the world's jungle. One morning, suddenly, there was silence from the nest; the fledglings had flown. A loneliness enveloped the writer's aerie, with its old army-green desk from Ninety-ninth Street, its tinny electric heaters, its bookshelves of raw pine attached to the studs with screwed-in L-brackets, its cardboard boxes of confused but accumulating manuscript. For Bech had, even before their Scots trip, taken root in his birdhouse; he had accepted Bea's advice and was pecking his way steadily through the ghostly tangle of *Think Big*.

Bech's fourth and, as critical diction has it, "long-awaited" novel existed in several spurts, or shoals, of inspiration. The first had come upon him in London, during a brief fling with a petite heiress and gossip columnist named Merissa, and took the envisioned form of an ambitious and elegiac novel directed, like *Anna Karenina* and *Madame Bovary*, toward the heroine's suicide. The heroine was to have Merissa's exquisite small bones and feline adaptability but to be squarely, winsomely, self-ruinously American. Her name came to him, with an oddness bespeaking a profoundly subconscious imperative, as Olive. Bech managed about sixty handwritten pages, dealing mostly with Olive's education at a Southern girls' college where the stench of horse manure incongruously swept through the curried green campus and the idyllic vista of young women of good family striding to class in smart skirts and high heels. But when it came time in the novel to bring her to that capital of ruined innocence, New York City, he was at a loss for what professional field he should mire her in. The only one he knew first-hand, that of publishing, inspired great distaste in our author when encountered in fiction; he did not much like involution, indeed, whether met in Escher prints, iris petals, or the romantic theme of incest. Yet all those glass boxes weighing on the heart of the city—what was done inside them, what empires rose and fell? He could not imagine. Stalled, Bech let a year slide by as he responded to invitations and filled out questionnaires from doctoral candidates. Then, one iron-cold winter afternoon, with steam pouring lavishly from the radiator valves, Bech to counter his claustrophobia turned on television, and met there a young actress's face uplifted beseechingly toward that of an aseptic-capped doctor, whose soothing baritone yet had a menacing rumble to it. Turning the channel, Bech eavesdropped upon the staccato conversation of two vexed women as they swiftly circulated among the furniture of a Texas-scale living room. Clicking past a channel of electronic ticker tape and another of Spanish sitcom, he found on the third major network a teen-aged girl screaming and snuffling about an abortion while California cliffs soared past the windows of her convertible. Here, Bech realized, was an empire, a kingdom as extensive and mystically ramified as a Chinese dynasty; the giant freckled figure of boyish, ruthless Tad Greenbaum swam into his cerebrum, trailing those of pliant, pill-popping Thelma Stern, Tad's mistress; her diabolical ex-husband, the enigmatic Polonius Stern; and her unscrupulous though insouciant lawyer-brother, Dolf Lessup. A world of searingly lighted soundstages and intimately dark cutting rooms, of men frantically reaching out from within a closed expensive world of glass desks and deep carpets and dim French restaurants toward the unseen millions sitting lonely in shabby rooms, offered itself to Bech as a wilderness sufficiently harsh to memorialize, and one wherein all his ignorances could be filled in with bits from those old Hollywood movies about making Hollywood movies. For some pages, his path lit alternately by klieg lights and *crêpes flambées*, the author moved through this luminous maze, until all lights failed and he went dry again. For the fact was that power, and the battle for it, utterly bored Bech. Then he met Ellen, a Steiner School teacher, and by the glow of her intelligent, unsmiling moon face he revised some of the yellowing old shoals. Olive, his heroine, became Lenore, and not so vulnerable and innocent as when she had been conceived, toward the end of the still-sexist Sixties. Today's young woman would sooner commit murder than suicide. And television soap opera had become, disconcertingly, the rage, a cliché. More trips mercifully intervened. Bech had passed fifty, and his hair had become a startling blob of white in the publicity photographs, and his work in progress, *Think Big*, had been so often mentioned in print that collectors wrote him in some exasperation over their inability to procure a copy. It was this mess of hopeful beginnings, it was this blasted dream, that Bea now ordered him to make come true.

What did she know of art? She had been an honors student at Vassar, majoring in economics. Her father, old Judge Latchett, recently dead, had run the quickest docket in the East. Her sister, the difficult Norma, ill-disguised prototype of Thelma Stern, had had a testy and judgmental tongue. Bea's softness, which had lured him, sheathed an instinctive efficiency; at heart she was still that good child who would check off Toothbrushing, Breakfast, and Toidy on the chart provided before going off each day to school. "Writing isn't like that," he protested.

"Like what?"

"Like toothbrushing and breakfast and doing toidy. The world doesn't need it that way."

She thought, her face in repose round and unsmiling, like that of his character Lenore. "*You* do, though," she said. "Need it. Because you're a writer. At least that's what you told me you were."

Bech ignored the suggestion that he had deceived her, for the many years of their courtship. He pursued his argument: "To justify its existence writing has to be extraordinary. If it's ordinary it's less than worthless; it's clutter. Go into any bookstore and try to breathe. You can't. Too many words produced by people working every morning."

"You know," Bea told him, "Rodney wasn't that crazy about being a bonds analyst, either. He would have loved to play tennis all day, every day. But up he got, to catch that 7:31, rain or shine; it used to break my heart. I'd hide in bed until he was gone, it made me feel so guilty."

"See," Bech said. "By marrying me, you've freed yourself from guilt." But every time she brandished Rodney's example at him, he knew that he had given the world of power a hook into his flesh.

"Donald keeps asking me what you *do*," Bea went on ruthlessly. "The girls were asked at school if it was true you were insane. I mean, thirteen years without a word."

"Now you're hurting me."

"You're hurting *us*," she said, her face going pink in patches. "Rodney feels sorry for me, I can tell over the phone."

"Oh *fuck* Rodney. What do I care about the Rodneys of the world? Why'd you ever leave him if he was so great?"

"He was a pill; but don't make me say it. It's you I love, obviously. Forget everything I said, I *love* it the way you keep yourself pure by never putting pen to paper. There's just one little thing."

"What's that?"

"Never mind."

"No, tell me." He loved secrets, had loved them ever since his father whispered to him that his mother was bad-tempered that day for a reason that had nothing to do with them, and that some day when Henry grew up he would understand. It was not until Bech was about thirty-eight, and lying in bed beside a lovely sleeping girl called Claire, that Bech realized his father had been referring to menstruation.

"We need the dough," Bea said.

"Oho. Now you're really talking."

"This is a big house to heat, and they say fuel oil's going to go to a dollar a gallon. And some slates fell off the north side after that big wind last week."

"Let's sell this barn and move back to the Apple, where the living is easy."

"You know I would, if it weren't for the children."

He knew nothing of the kind, but enjoyed making her lie. He enjoyed, indeed, these contentious conversations, bringing out the Norma in Bea, and would have continued had not the front-door bell rung. It was Marcie Flint, another driven veteran of the suburban quotidian, come to compare second marriages over coffee. Bech fled upstairs, past all the tumbled toys and blankets of the children's bedrooms, to his third-floor retreat. He scratched out *Think Big* on page one of his mauled manuscript and penned the words *Easy Money*. He changed his heroine's name back to Olive. Ripe with reckless scorn, he began anew.

As Bech typed, countering with his four-finger syncopation the nervous rustling of the Rodentia overhead, and as spring's chartreuse buds and melting breezes yielded to the oppressive overgrowth of summer, in turn to be dried and tinted according to the latest fall fashions and returned to the frostbound earth, memories of Manhattan weather washed through him unpredictably, like pangs of bursitis. There, the seasons spoke less in the flora of the hard-working parks than in the costumes of the human fauna, the furs and wool and leather boots and belts and the summer cotton and clogs and in these recent condition-conscious years the shimmering tanktops and supershorts of the young women who rose up from the surfaces of stone as tirelessly as flowers out of mud. New York was so *sexy*, in memory: the indoorness of it all, amid circumambient peril, and the odd good health imposed upon everyone by the necessity of hiking great distances in the search for taxis, of struggling through revolving doors and lugging bags heavy with cheesecake and grapefruit up and down stairs, the elevator being broken. On this island of primitive living copulation occurred as casually as among Polynesians, while Scarlatti pealed from the stereo and the garbage truck whined its early-morning song two blocks away. Bech remembered, from that cozy long decade of his life before the onset of Claire, how he had gone home from a publishing party with a *Mademoiselle* editor and how in her narrow kitchen her great silvery breasts had spilled from her loosened Shantung dress into his hands as simultaneously their mouths fused in the heat of first kiss and his eyes, furtively sneaking a look at his surroundings, filled with the orbs of the glossy red onions hung on a jutting nail above this overflowing lady's sink. He remembered how Claire, slender as a fish, would flit naked through the aquarium light of his own rooms as a short winter day ended outside in a flurry of wet snow collecting flake by flake on the ridges of the fire escape. She had been studying dance in those remote days, and in the dimness as Ravel latticed the air with rhythm could have been practicing in a flesh-colored leotard but for the vertical smudge of her pubic hair; unlike the dark triangle that was standard her pussy formed a gauzy little column as of smoke. Of the mistress succeeding Claire, Bech entertained fewer nostalgic memories, for she had been Norma Latchett, now his sister-in-law. Norma occasionally visited them, dirtying every ashtray in the house with a single lipsticky cigarette each and exuding a rapacious melancholy that penetrated to Bech even through the dungeon walls of the kinship taboo that now prevailed between them. Judge Latchett, having sent so many to their reward, had gone to his, and the sisters' mother was legally incompetent; so Norma now faintly stank to Bech of family depressingness, as Wasps know it. It was the romantic period before Norma that with a sweetness bordering on pain welled up to flood the blank spaces in his ragged manuscript; it now seemed a marvel worth confiding that through those publicly convulsed years under two lugubrious presidents the nation had contained catacombs of private life. Bech at his green steel desk retrieved that vast subterrain detail by detail and interwove the overheard music of a tranced time with the greedy confusion his characters bred. They were, but for Olive and some lesser *shikse* mistresses, Jewish, and here, in this house built and repeatedly bought by Protestants, and presently occupied save for himself by blonds, and haunted by the tight-lipped ghost of Rodney Cook, Jewishness too became a kind of marvel—a threadbare fable still being spun, an energy and irony vengefully animating the ruins of Christendom, a flavor and guile and humor and inspired heedlessness truly superhuman, a spectacle elevated the promised Biblical notch above the rest of the human drama. His own childhood, his Brooklyn uncles and West Side upbringing, he now saw, through the precious wrong end of the telescope, to be as sharp and toylike as once the redneck motorcyclists of the Midwest had seemed, when the telescope was pointed in the other direction. Day by day his imagination caught slow fire and smoldered a few pages to the gray of type-script. He had determined not to rewrite, in his usual patient-spider style, or even to reread, except to check the color of a character's hair or sports car. Where the events seemed implausible, he reasoned that a novel about Greenbaum Productions might legitimately have the tex-ture of a soap opera; where a character seemed thin and unformed, he reassured himself that later episodes would flesh him out; where a gap loomed, Bech enshrined yet another erotic memory from that past enchanted by the removes of time and his Ossining exile. He cast off as spiritual patrons finicky Flaubert and Kafka and adopted the pragmatic fatalism of those great native slapdashers Melville and Faulkner. Whatever faults he was bundling pell-mell into his opus he saw as deepening his revenge upon Bea. For his uncharacteristic gallop of activity was among other things spiteful—fulfillment of a vow to "show" her. "I'll show you!" children would sometimes shout, near tears, beneath his window.

Downstairs, when the day's dizzying flight with the smirched angels of his imagining was over, a brave new domestic world awaited Bech. For lunch he might eat several drying peanut-butter-and-jelly sandwich halves that Donald and a playmate had spurned an hour before. As summer ripened, vegetables from Bea's garden—beans, broccoli, zucchini—might be lying on the butcher-block kitchen counter and could be nibbled raw. That there was great nutritional and moral benefit in raw, home-grown vegetables was one of the Christian notions he found piquant. If Bea was around, she might warm him soup from a can and sit at the round kitchen table and sip some with him. Luncheon meat might be in the refrigerator or not, depending upon the vagaries of her shopping and the predations of Ann's and Judy's boyfriends. It was a contrast of chaos to the provender of Bech's bachelor days, when the stack of delicatessen salami occupying in lonely splendor the second shelf of his refrigerator went down at the inexorable rate of three slices a day, like a book being slowly read through. Dinner in those days he usually ate out; or else, in the emergency of a blizzard or an irresistible TV special, he heated up a frozen Chinese meal, the heart of the egg roll still deliciously icy. Here, wed, he confronted great formal meals planned by Bea as if to fatten him up for the kill, or else fought for scraps with barbaric adolescents.

Ann's and Judy's boyfriends struck him as a clamorous and odorous swarm of dermatological disasters, a pack of howling wolves clad in the latest style of ragbag prep, their clothes stretching and ripping under the pressure of their growing bodies, their modes of courtship uniformly impossible to ignore, from the demonstrations of football prowess arranged on the September lawn to the post-midnight spinouts of their parents' Mercedeses on the gravel drive after some vernal dance. The twin girls themselves—Ann a touch more pensive and severe than Judy, Judy the merest shade more womanly than Ann, as if the fifteen minutes by which she had preceded her into the world insured an everlasting edge of maturity—were

much at school. Bech was irritably conscious of their
presence most during those evenings when, bored by
homework, they would collapse together into whispering
and giggles, making in the house an everywhere audible,
bottomless vortex of female hilarity that fed endlessly
upon itself and found fresh cause wherever it glanced.
Bech could only imagine that he was somehow the joke,
and feared that the entire house and his life with it would
be sucked down into their insatiable mirth, so sinisterly
amplified by twinnishness. Whereas little Donald, his
companion in the error of being male, stirred in him only
tender feelings. In the child's clumsy warrior energy he
saw himself at heart; standing above the sleeping boy's
bed at night, he took the measure of his own grotesque
age and, by the light of this dream-flushed, perfect
cheek, his own majestic corruption. Donald returned on
the pumpkin-colored school bus around four, and sometimes he and Bech would play catch with a baseball or
football, the forgotten motions returning strangely to
Bech's shoulders, the rub and whack of leather to his
hands. Or, before the fall chill caused the backyard pools
to be drained and the tarpaulins tugged into place, the
two of them and Bea might go swimming at a neighbor's
place to which Bea's old friendship gave them access, and
where the hostess would emerge to keep them company
and offer them a drink. These old friends of Bea's, named
Wryson or Weed or Hake or Crutchman—sharp English
names that might have come off the roster of a sailing
ship—had their charms and no doubt their passions and
disappointments and histories, but seemed so exotic to
Bech, so brittle and pale and complacently situated amid

their pools and dogwoods and the old Dutch masonry of their retaining walls, that he felt like a spy among them and, when not a silent spy, a too-vigorous, curly-haired showoff. Exquisite and languid as a literary practitioner, he was made to feel among Bea's people vulgar and muscular, a Marx brother about to pull up a skirt or grind out a cigar in a finger bowl. An evening amid such expectations wearied him. "I don't know," he sighed to Bea. "They're just not my crowd."

"You don't give them a chance," she said, driving him home along the winding lanes. "You think just because they don't live in apartment houses and have metal bookcases crammed to the ceilings and grandparents that came from a *shtetl* they're not people. But Louise Bentley, that you met tonight, had something really terrible happen to her years ago, and Johnny Hake, though I know he can get carried away, really *did* pull himself back from the abyss."

"I don't doubt," Bech said. "But it's not my abyss." Money, for example, as these Wasps possessed it, seemed something rigid and invisible, like glass. Though it could be broken and distributed, acquired and passed on, it quite lacked organic festiveness. Whereas money under Jewish hands was yeasty; it grew and spread and frolicked on the counting table. And their bizarre, Christmassy religion: many of Bea's crowd went to church, much as they faithfully played tennis and golf and attended rallies to keep out developers. Yet their God, for all of His colorful history and spangled attributes, lay above Earth like a whisper of icy cirrus, a tenuous and diffident Other Whose tendrils failed to entwine with

fibrous blood and muscle; whereas the irrepressible Jewish God, the riddle of joking rabbis, playing His practical jokes upon Job and Abraham and leading His chosen
into millennia of mire without so much as the promise
of an afterlife, this God beside Whom even the many-
armed deities of the Hindus appeared sleek and plausible,
nevertheless entered into the daily grind and kibitzed at
all transactions. Being among the goyim frightened Bech,
in truth; their collective chill was the chill of devils.

He felt easier in downtown Ossining, with its basking
blacks and its rotting commercial streets tipped down
sharply toward the Hudson and its chunky Gothic brick-
and-cornice architecture whispering to Bech's fancy of
robber barons and fairy tales and Washington Irving.
Washington Heights, he supposed, once looked much as
Ossining did now. He had not expected such a strong
dark-skinned presence on the streets so far up the Hudson, or the slightly sleepy Southern quality of it all—
the vacant storefronts, the idle wharfs, the clapboarded
shacks and rusting railroad spurs and Civil War memo-
rials. Throughout the northeastern United States, he
realized, there were towns like this, perfected long ago
and filled with ice cream and marching music, only to
slide into a sunstruck somnolence, like flecks of pyrite
weeping rusty stain from the face of a granite escarp-
ment. Ossining, he learned, was a euphemism; in 1901, the
village fathers had changed the name from Sing Sing,
which had been pre-empted by the notorious prison and
long ago had been stolen from the Indians, in whose
Mohican language "Sin Sinck" meant "stone upon stone."
Stone upon stone the vast correctional facility had arisen;

electrocutions here used to dim the lights for miles around, according to the tabloids Bech read as a boy. The coarsely screened newspaper photos of the famed "hot seat" at Sing Sing, and the movie scene wherein Cagney is dragged, moaning and rubbery-legged, down a long corridor to his annihilation, had told the young Bech all he ever wanted to know about death. He wondered if denizens of the underworld still snarled at one another, "You'll fry for this," and supposed not. The lights of Ossining no longer dimmed in sympathy with snuffed-out murderers. The folks downtown looked merry to Bech, and the whole burg on a play scale; he had the true New Yorker's secret belief that people living anywhere else had to be, in some sense, kidding. On that sloping stage between Peekskill and Tarrytown he enjoyed being enrolled in the minor-city minstrelsy; he often volunteered to run Bea's errands for household oddments, killing time in the long dark unair-conditioned drugstore, coveting the shine on the paperbacks by Uris and Styron and marvelling at the copious cosmetic innocence of commercial America. His light-headedness on these away-from-home afternoons strengthened him to burrow on, through that anfractuous fantasy he was weaving among the lost towers of Gotham.

He remembered the great city in the rain, those suddenly thrashing downpours flash-flooding the asphalt arroyos and overflowing the grated sewer mains, causing citizens to huddle—millionaires and their mistresses companionable with bag ladies and messenger boys—under restaurant canopies and in the recessed marble portals of

international banks, those smooth fortresses of hidden
empire. In such a rain, Tad Greenbaum and Thelma
Stern are caught without their limousine. For some time,
remember, Thelma has been resolved to leave Tad but
dreads and postpones the moment of announcement. The
taxis splash past, their little cap lights doused, their back
seats holding the shadowy heads of those mysterious per-
sonages who find cabs in the worst of weathers: when
the nuclear weapons begin to fall, these same shadows
will be fleeing the city in perfect repose, meters ticking.
Thelma's dainty Delman's, high gold heels each held to
her feet by a single gilded ankle strap, become so soaked
as she wades through the gutter's black rivulet that she
takes them off, and then scampers across the shining tar
in her bare feet. No, cross that out, her feet are not bare,
she would be wearing pantyhose; with a madcap impulse
she halts, beneath the swimming DONT WALK sign, and
reaches up into her Shantung skirt and peels herself free,
disentangling first the left leg, then the right. Now her
feet are truly bare. Tomboyishly she, who as the lithe
Lessup girl had run wild in the hills of Kentucky, wads
the drenched nylon and chucks it overhand into one of
those UFO-like trash barrels the filth-beleaguered me-
tropolis provides. Tad, catching up to her, his size thirteen iguana-skin penny loafers still soggily in place,
laughs aloud at her reckless gesture. Her gold shoes
follow into the bin; his immense freckled baritone rings
out into the tumult of water and taxi tires and squeal-
ing hookers caught loitering in their scarlet stretch
pants a few doors up Third Avenue with no more for

shelter than a MASSAGE PARLOR sign. "I—want—*out*,"
she suddenly shouts up at him. Her raven hair is pasted
about her fine skeletal face like the snake-ringlets of
Medusa.

"Out—of—*what?*" Tad thunders back.

Still the pedestrian sign says DONT WALK, though the
traffic light on the avenue has turned red. The ghostly
pallor of her face, upturned toward his in the streaming
rain, takes on an abrupt greenish tinge. "Out—of—*you*,"
she manages to shout at last, the leap of her life, her heart
falling sickeningly within her at the utterance; Tad's face
looms above her like a blimp, bloated and unawares, his
chestnut mop flattened on his wide freckled brow and
releasing down one temple a thin tan trickle of the color-
freshener his hair stylist favors. He is just a boy growing
old, she thinks to herself, with a boy's warrior brutality,
and a boy's essential ignorance. Without such ignorance,
how could men act? How could they create empires, or
for that matter cross the street?

Their sign has changed from red to white, a blur spelling perilously WALK. Tad and Thelma run across Third
Avenue to take refuge in the shallow arcade of a furrier.
The street surface is a rippling film; wrappers are
bunched at the clogged corner grate like bridesmaids'
handkerchiefs. Feeling tar on the soles of her feet and
being pelted by rain all the length of her naked calves has
released in Thelma an elemental self which scorns Tad
and his charge cards and his tax breaks. He, on the other
hand, his Savile Row suit collapsed against his flesh and an
absurd succession of droplets falling from the tip of his

nose, looks dismal and crazed. "You bitch," he says to her in the altered acoustics of this dry spot. "You're not going to pull this put-up-or-shut-up crap again; you know it's just a matter of time."

Meaning, she supposes, until he leaves Ginger—Ginger Greenbaum, that stubborn little pug of a wife, always wearing caftans and muu-muus to hide her thirty pounds of overweight. Thelma marvels at herself, that she could ever sleep with a man who sleeps with that spoiled and pouting parody of a woman, whose money (made by her father in meatpacking) had fed Tad's infant octopus. It seems comic. She laughs, and prods with a disrespectful forefinger the man's drenched shirtfront of ribbed Egyptian cotton. His stomach is spongy; there comes by contrast into her mind the taut body of her slender Olive, their gentle mutual explorations in that exiguous, triangular West Side apartment where the light from New Jersey enters as horizontally as bars of music and overlays with such long shadows the breathing silence of the two intertwined women.

Tad slugs her. Or, rather, cuffs her shoulder, since she saw it coming and flinched; the blow bumps her into a wire burglar-guard behind which a clay-faced mannequin preens in an ankle-length burnoose lined with chinchilla. The rain has lessened, the golden taxis going by are all empty. "You were thinking of that other bitch," Tad has shrewdly surmised.

"I was not," Thelma fervently lies, determined now to protect at all costs that slender other, that stranger to their city; she has remembered how the subtle crests of

Olive's ilia cast horizontal shadows across her flat, faintly undulant abdomen. "Let's go back to your place and get dry," she suggests.

And Henry Bech in his mind's eye saw the drying streets, raggedly dark as if after a storm of torn carbon paper, and each grate exuding a vapor indistinguishable from leaks of municipal steam. And the birds, with that unnoticed bliss of New York birds, have begun to sing, to sing from every pocket park and potted curbside shrub, while sunlight wanly resumes and Thelma—all but her sloe eyes and painted fingernails hidden within the rustling, iridescent cumulus of a bubble bath in Tad's great sunken dove-colored tub—begins to cry. It is a good feeling, like champagne in the sinuses. His own sinuses prickling, Bech lifted his eyes and read the words *Apply this side toward living space* on the aluminum-foil backing of his room's insulation. He turned his attention out the window toward the lawn, where little Donald and a grubby friend were gouging holes in the mowed grass to make a miniature golf course. Bech thought of yelling at them from his height but decided it wasn't his lawn, his world; his world was here, with Tad and Thelma. She emerges from the bathroom drying herself with a russet towel the size of a Ping-Pong-table top. "You big pig," she tells Tad with that self-contempt of women which is their dearest and darkest trait, "I love your shit." He in his silk bathrobe is setting out on his low glass Mies table—no, it is a round coffee table with a leather center and a stout rim of oak, and carved oaken legs with griffin feet—champagne glasses and, in a little silver eighteenth-century salt dish bought at auction at

Sotheby's, the white, white cocaine. Taxi horns twinkle far below. Thelma sits—whether in bald mockery of the impending fuck or to revisit that sensation of barefoot mountain-girl uncontrollability she had experienced on the rainswept street, it would take a psychologist and not a mere novelist to discern—naked on an ottoman luxuriously covered in zebra hide. Each hair is a tiny needle. Bech shifted from buttock to buttock in his squeaking chair, empathizing.

By such reckless daily fits, as seven seasons slowly wheeled by in the woods and gardens of Ossining, the manuscript accumulated: four emptied boxes of bond paper were needed to contain it, and still the world set forth seemed imperfectly explored, a cave illumined by feeble flashlight, with ever more incidents and vistas waiting behind this or that stalagmite, or just on the shadowy far shore of the unstirring alkaline pool. At night sometimes he would read Bea a few pages of it, and she would nod beside him in bed, exhaling the last drag of her cigarette (she had taken up smoking, after years on the nicotine wagon, in what mood of renewed desperation or fresh anger he could not fathom), and utter crisply, "It's good, Henry."

"That's all you can say?"

"It's loose. You're really rolling. You've gotten those people just where you want them."

"Something about the way you say that—"

"Well what am I supposed to do, whoop for joy?" She doused her butt with a vehement hiss in the paper bathroom cup half-full of water she kept by her bedside in lieu of an ashtray, a trick learned at Vassar. "All those old sugarplums you fucked in New York, do you really think I enjoy hearing about how great they were?"

"Honey, it's *fan*tasy. I never knew anybody like these people. These people have money. The people I knew all subscribed to *Commentary*, before it went fascist."

"Do you realize there isn't a Gentile character in here who isn't slavishly in love with some Jew?"

"Well, that's—"

"Well, that's life, you're going to say."

"Well, that's the kind of book it is. *Travel Light* was *all* about Gentiles."

"Seen as hooligans. As barbaric people. How can you think that, living two years now with Ann and Judy and Donald? He just adores you, you know that, don't you?"

"He can beat me at Battleship, that's what he likes. Hey, are you crying?"

She had turned her head away. She rattled at her night table, lighting another cigarette with her back still turned. The very space of the room had changed, as if their marriage had passed through a black hole and come out as anti-matter. Bea prolonged the operation, knowing she had roused guilt in him, and when she at last turned back gave him a profile as cool as the head on a coin. She had a toughness, Bea, that the toughness of her sister, Norma, had long eclipsed but that connubial solitude revealed. "I've another idea for your title," she said, biting off the words softly and precisely. "Call it *Jews and Those Awful Others*. Or how about *Jews and Jerks*?"

Bech declined to make the expected protest. What he

minded most about her in these moods was his sense of being programmed, of being fitted tightly into a pattern of reaction; she wanted, his loving suburban softy, to *nail him down.*

Frustrated by his silence, she conceded him her full face, her eyes rubbed pink in the effort of suppressing tears and her mouth a blurred cloud of flesh-color sexier than any lipstick. She put an arm about him. He reciprocated, careful of the cigarette close to his ear. "I just thought," she confessed, her voice coming in little heated spurts of breath, "your living here so long now with me, with *us*, something nice would get into your book. But those people are so vicious, Henry. There's no love making them tick, just ego and greed. Is that how you see us? I mean us, people?"

"No, no," he said, patting, thinking that indeed he did, indeed he did.

"I recognize these gestures and bits of furniture you've taken from your life here, but it doesn't seem at all like me. This idiotic Ginger character, I hate her, yet sometimes whole sentences I know I've said come out of her mouth."

He stroked the roundness of the shoulder that her askew nightie strap bared, while her solvent tears, running freely, released to his nostrils the scent of discomposed skin moisturizer. "The only thing you and Ginger Greenbaum have in common," he assured her, "is you're both married to beasts."

"You're not a beast, you're a dear kind man—"

"Away from my desk," he interjected.

"—but I get the feeling when you read your book to

me it's a way of paying me *back*. For loving you. For marrying you."

"Who was it," he asked her, "who told me to do a few pages a day and not worry about *le mot juste* and the capacity for taking infinite pains and all that crap? Who?"

"Please don't be so angry," Bea begged. The hand of the arm not around his shoulders and holding a cigarette, the hand of the arm squeezed between and under their facing tangent bodies, found his dormant prick and fumblingly enclosed it. "I love your book," she said. "Those people are so silly and wild. Not like us at all. Poor little Olive."

His voice softened as his prick hardened. "You talk as though this was the first time I've ever written about Jews. That's not so. *Brother Pig* had that union organizer in it, and there were even rabbis in *The Chosen*. I just didn't want to do what all the others were doing, and what Singer had done in Yiddish anyway."

She snuffled, quite his Christian maiden now, and burrowed her pink nose deeper into the grizzly froth of his chest while her touch lower down took on a quicksilver purity and slidingness. "I have a terrible confession to make," she said. "I never got through *The Chosen*. It was assigned years ago in a reading group I belonged to up here, and I tried to read it, and kept getting interrupted, and then the group discussed it and it was as if I *had* read it."

Any guilt Bech might have been feeling toward her eased. Claire had read *The Chosen*; it had been dedicated to her. Norma had read it twice, taking notes. He rolled across Bea's body and switched off the light. "Nobody who did read it liked it," he said in the dark, and kneeled above her, near her face.

"Wait," she said, and dunked her cigarette with a sizzle. Something like a wet smoke ring encircled him; tightened, loosened. What beasts we all are. What pigs, Thelma would say. *I love your shit.*

Bea found him a typist—Mae, a thirty-year-old black woman with an IBM Selectric in a little ranch house the color of faded raspberries on Shady Lane; there was a green parakeet in a cage and a small brown child hiding behind every piece of furniture. Bech was afraid Mae wouldn't be able to spell, but as it turned out she was all precision and copyediting punctilio; she was in rebellion against her racial stereotype, like a Chinese rowdy or an Arab who hates to haggle. It was frightening, seeing his sloppily battered-out, confusingly revised manuscript go off and come back the next weekend as stacks of crisp prim typescript, with a carbon on onionskin and a separate pink sheet of queried corrigenda. He was being edged closer to the dread plunge of publication, as when, younger, he would mount in a line of shivering wet children to the top of the great water slide at Coney Island—a shaky little platform a mile above turquoise depths that still churned after swallowing their last victim—and the child behind him would nudge the backs of his legs, when all Bech wanted was to stand there a while and think about it.

"Maybe," he said to Bea, "since Mae is such a whiz, and must need the money—you never see a husband around the place, just that parakeet—I should go over it once more and have her retype."

"Don't you dare," Bea said.

"But you've said yourself, you loathe the book. Maybe I can soften it. Take out that place where the video crew masturbates all over Olive's drugged body, put in a scene where they all come up to Ossining and admire the fall foliage." Autumn had invaded their little woods with its usual glorious depredations. Bech had begun to work in his insulated room two springs ago. Spring, summer, fall, winter, spring, summer, fall: those were the seven seasons he had labored, while little Donald turned twelve and Ann, so Judy had tattled, lost her virginity.

"I loathe it, but it's you," Bea said. "Show it to your publisher."

This was most frightening. Fifteen years had passed since he had submitted a manuscript to The Vellum Press. In this interval the company had been sold to a supermarket chain who had peddled it to an oil company who had in turn, not liking the patrician red of Vellum's bottom line, managed to foist the firm off on a West Coast lumber-and-shale-based conglomerate underwritten, it was rumored, by a sinister liaison of Japanese and Saudi money. It was like being a fallen woman in the old days: once you sold yourself, you were never your own again. But at each change of ownership, Bech's books, *outré* enough to reassure the public that artistic concerns had not been wholly abandoned, were reissued in a new paperback format. His long-time editor at Vellum, dapper, sensitive Ned Clavell, had succumbed to well-earned cirrhosis of the liver and gone to that three-martini luncheon in the sky. Big Billy Vanderhaven, who had founded the firm as a rich man's plaything in the days of the trifling tax bite and who had concocted its name loosely out of his own, had long since retired to Hawaii, where he lived with his fifth wife on a diet of seaweed and macadamia nuts. A great fadster, who had raced at Le Mans and mountain-climbed in Nepal and scuba-dived off Acapulco, "Big" Billy—so called sixty years ago to distinguish him from his effete and once socially prominent cousin, "Little" Billy Vanderhaven—had apparently cracked the secret of eternal life, which is Do Whatever You Please. Yet, had the octogenarian returned under the sponsorship of that Japanese and Saudi money to take the helm of Vellum again, the effect could have been scarcely less sensational than Henry Bech turning up with a new manuscript. Bech no longer knew the name of anyone at the firm except the woman who handled permissions and sent him his little checks and courtesy copies of relevant anthologies, with their waxen covers and atrocious typos. When at last, gulping and sitting down and shutting his eyes and preparing to slide, he dialled Vellum's number, it was the editor-in-chief he asked for. He was connected to the snotty voice of a boy.

"You're the editor-in-chief?" he asked incredulously.

"No I am not," the voice said, through its nose. "This is her secretary."

"Oh. Well could I talk to her?"

"May I ask who is calling, please?"

Bech told him.

"Could you spell that, please?"

"Like the beer but with an 'h' on the end like in 'Heineken.' "

"Truly? Well aren't we boozy this morning!"

There was a cascade of electronic peeping, a cup-shaped silence, and then a deep female voice saying, "Mr. Schlitzeh?"

"No, no. Bech. B-E-C-H. Henry. I'm one of your authors."

"You sure are. Absolutely. It's an honor and a pleasure to hear your voice. I first read you in Irvington High School; they assigned *Travel Light* to the accelerated track. It knocked me for a loop. And it's stayed with me. Not to mention those others. What can I do for you, sir? I'm Doreen Pease, by the way. Sorry we've never met."

From all this Bech gathered that he was something of a musty legend in the halls of Vellum, and that nevertheless here was a busy woman with her own gravity and attested velocity and displacement value. He should come to the point. "I'm sorry, too," he began.

"I *wish* we could get you in here for lunch some time. I'd love to get your slant on the new format we've given your reprints. We're just crazy about what this new designer has done, she's *just* out of the Rhode Island School of Design, but those stick figures against those electric colors, with the sateen finish, and the counterstamped embossing—"

"Stunning," Bech agreed.

"You know, it gives a *un*ity; for me it gives the shopper a handle on what *you* are all about, you as opposed to each individual title. The salesmen report that the chains have been really enthusiastic: some of them have given us a week in the window. And that ain't just hay, for quality softcover."

"Well, actually, Mrs.—Miss?—Miz?—"

"Doreen will do fine."

"It's about a book I'm calling."

"Yess?" That was it, a single spurt of steam, impatient. The pleasantries were over, the time clock was running.

"I've written a new one and wondered whom I should send it to."

The silence this time was not cup-shaped, but more like that of a liqueur glass, narrow and transparent, with a brittle stem.

She said, "When you say you've written it, what do you mean exactly? This isn't an outline, or a list of chapters, you want us to bid on?"

"No, it's finished. I mean, there may be some revisions on the galleys—"

"The first-pass proofs, yess."

"Whatever. And as to the bid, in the old days, when Big—when Mr. Vanderhaven was around, you'd just take it, and print it, and pay me a royalty we thought was fair."

"Those *were* the old days," Doreen Pease said, permitting herself a guffaw, and what sounded like a puff on her cigar. "Let's get our dominoes all in line, Mr. Bech. You've finished a manuscript. Is this the *Think Big* you mention in interviews from time to time?"

"Well, the title's been changed, tentatively. My wife, I'm married now—"

"I read that in *People*. About six months ago, wasn't it?"

"Two and a half years, actually. My wife had this theory about how to write a book. You just sit down—"

"And do it. Well of course. Smart girl. And you're calling me to ask who to send it to? Where's your agent in all this?"

He blushed—a wasted signal over the phone. "I've never had one. I hate people reading over my shoulder."

"Henry, I'm cutting my own throat saying this, but if I were you I'd get me one. Starting now. A book by Henry Bech is a major development. But if you want to play it your way, send it straight here to me. Doreen Pease. Like the vegetable with an 'e' on the end."

"Or I could bring it down on the train. I seem to live up here in Westchester."

"Tell me where and we'll send a messenger in a limo to pick it up."

He told her where and asked, "Isn't a limo expensive?"

"We find it cuts way down on postage and saves us a fortune in the time sector. Anyway, let's face it, Henry: you're top of the line. What'd you say the title was?"

"*Easy Money*."

"Oh yesss."

The hiss sounded prolonged. He wondered if he was tiring her. "Uh, one more thing, Miss Pease, Doreen. If it turns out you like it and want to print it—"

"Oh, Christ, I'm sure we'll want to, it can't be that terrible. You're very sweetly modest, Henry, but you have a name, and names don't grow on trees these days; television keeps coming up with so many new celebrities the public has lost track. The public is a conservative animal: that's the conclusion I've come to after twenty years in this business. They like the tried and true. You'd know that better than I would." She guffawed; she had decided that he was somehow joshing her, and that all her worldly wisdom was his also.

"What I wanted to ask," Bech said, "was would I be assigned an editor? My old one, Ned Clavell, died a few years ago."

"He was a bit before my era here, but I've heard a ton about him. He must have been a wonderful man."

"He had his points. He cared a lot about not splitting infinitives or putting too much vermouth into a martini."

"Yess. I think I know what you're saying. I'm reading you, Henry."

She was? He seemed to hear her humming; but perhaps it was another conversation fraying into this line.

"I think in that case," Doreen decided, "we better give you over to our Mr. Flaggerty. He's young, but very brilliant. *Very*. And sensitive. He knows when to *stop*, is I think the quality you'll most appreciate. Jim's a delicious person, I *know* you'll be *very* happy with him."

"I don't have to be *that* happy," Bech said, but in a burble of electronic exclamations their connection was broken off. Neither party felt it necessary to re-place the call.

The limo arrived at five. A young man with acne and a neo-Elvis wet look crawled out of the back and gave both Ann and Judy, who crowded into the front hall, a lecherous goggle eye. Bech began to fear that he was guarding treasure, with these blooming twins. Rodney, their biological father, after a period of angry mourning for his marriage, had descended into the mid-Manhattan dating game and exerted an ever feebler paternal presence. He showed up Sundays and took Donald to the

Bronx Zoo or a disaster movie, and that was about it. The only masculine voices the children heard in the house belonged to Bech and the old man who came in a plastic helmet to read the water meter. But now that his book was submitted and, as of November, "in the works," the homely mock-Tudor house tucked against the woods no longer felt like a hermitage. Calls from Vellum's publicity and production departments shrilled at the telephone, and a dangerous change in the atmosphere, like some flavorless pernicious gas, trickled through the foundation chinks into the heated waste spaces of their home: Bech, again a working author, was no longer quite the man Bea had married, or the one his stepchildren had become accustomed to.

Vellum Press (the "The" had been dropped during a streamlining operation under one of its former corporate owners) had its offices on the top six floors of a new Lexington Avenue skyscraper the lacteal white of ersatz-ivory piano keys; the architect, a Rumanian defector famous in the gossip press for squiring the *grandes dames* of the less titled jet set, had used every square inch of the building lot but given the skyline a fillip at the top, with a round pillbox whose sweeping windows made the publisher's offices feel like an airport control tower. When Bech had first published with Vellum in 1955, a single brownstone on East Sixty-seventh Street had housed the operation. In those days Big Billy himself, ruddy from outdoor sport, sat enthroned in a leather wing chair in what had been two fourth-floor maid's rooms, the partition broken through. He would toy with a Himalayan paper-knife and talk about his travels, his mountain-climbing and marlin-fishing, and about his losing battle with the greed and grossly decayed professional standards of printers. Bech enjoyed these lectures from on high, and felt exhilarated when they were over and he was released to the undogmatic, ever fresh street reality of the ginkgos, of the polished nameplates on the other brownstones, of the lean-legged women in mink jackets walking their ornamentally trimmed poodles. Ned Clavell's office had been a made-over scullery in the basement; from its one narrow window Bech could see these same dogs lift a fluffy hind leg, exposing a mauve patch of raw poodle, and daintily urinate on the iron fencing a few yards away. Ned had been a great fusser, to whom every page of prose gave a certain pain, which he politely tried to conceal, or to explain with maximum politeness, his hands showing a tremor as they shuffled sheets of manuscript, his handsome face pale with the strain of a hangover or of language's inexhaustible imperfection. His voice had had that hurried briskness of Thirties actors, of Ronald Colman and George Brent, and meticulously he had rotated his gray, brown, and blue suits, saving a double-breasted charcoal pinstripe for evening wear. A tiny gold rod had pressed the knot of his necktie out and the points of his shirt collar down; he wore rings on both hands, and had never married. Bech wondered now if he had been a homosexual; somehow not marrying in those years could seem a simple inadvertence, the omission of a dedicated man. "Piss off, you bitch!" he used to blurt out, from beneath his pencil-line mustache, when one of the poodles did its duty; and it took years for Bech to realize that Ned did not mean the dog but the woman with taut nylon ankles who was overseeing the little sparkling event. Yet Ned had been especially pained by Bech's fondness for the earthier American idioms, and they spent more than one morning awkwardly bartering tits, as it were, for tats, the editor's sharpened pencil silently pointing after a while at words he took no relish in pronouncing. Dear dead Ned: Bech sensed at the time he had his secret sorrows, his unpublished effusions and his unvented appetites, but the young author was set upon his own ambitions and used the other man as coolly as he used the mailman. Now the man was gone, taking his decent, double-breasted era with him.

Through the great bowed pane of Mr. Flaggerty's office the vista of the East River and of Queens' waterfront industrial sheds was being slowly squeezed away by rising new construction. Flaggerty also was tall, six three at least, and the hand he extended was all red-knuckled bones. He wore blue jeans and an open-necked shirt of the checkered sort that Bech associated with steelworkers out on their bowling night. He wondered, *How does this man take his authors to restaurants?* "It's super Doreen is letting me handle you," Flaggerty said.

"I've been told I'm hard to handle."

"Not the way I hear it. The old-timers I talk to say you're a pussycat."

This young man had an uncanny dreamy smile and seemed content to sit forever at his glass desk smiling, tipped back into his chair so that his knees were thrust up to the height of his stacked In and Out baskets. His lengthy pale face was assembled all of knobs, melted together; his high brow especially had a bumpy shine. His desk top looked empty and there was no telling what he was thinking as he gazed so cherishingly at Bech.

Bech asked him, "Have you read the book?"

"Every fucking word," Flaggerty said, as if this was unusual practice.

"And—?"

"It knocked me out. A real page-turner. Funny *and* gory."

"You have any suggestions?"

Flaggerty's wispy eyebrows pushed high into his forehead, multiplying the bumps. "No. Why would I?"

"The language didn't strike you as—a bit rough in spots?" One of Ned Clavell's favorite phrases.

This idea seemed doubly startling. "No, of course not. For me, it all worked. It went with the action."

"The scene with Olive and the video crew—"

"Gorgeous. Raunchy as hell, of course, but with, you know, a lot of crazy tenderness underneath. That's the kind of thing you do so well, Mr. Bech. Mind if I call you Henry?"

"Not at all. Sock it to me, Jim." Bech still had not got what he wanted—an unambiguous indication that this fellow had pondered the manuscript. He had the strange sensation, talking to Flaggerty, that his editor had not so much read the book as inhaled it: that Bech's book had been melted down and evaporated in these slice-of-pie-shaped offices and sent into the ozone to join the former contents of aerosol cans. Here, in Vellum's curved and pastel halls, languidly drifting young women in Vampira makeup outnumbered any signs of literary industry; the bulletin boards were monopolized by tampon and lingerie ads torn out of magazines, with all their chauvinistic implications underlined and annotated in indignant slashing felt-tip. Flaggerty's walls were white and mostly blank, but for a grainy blowup of Thomas Wolfe about to board a trolley car. Otherwise they might be sitting in a computer lab. Bech asked him, "How do you like the title?"

"*Easy Money*?" So he had got that far. "Not bad. Might confuse people a little, with all these how-to-get-rich-in-the-coming-crash books on the market."

"The original title was *Think Big*, but I found it hard to work under. I couldn't get going really until my wife told me to scrap the title."

"*Think Big*, huh?" Flaggerty's eyes, deep in their sockets of bone, widened. "I like it." They were beryl: an acute pale cat color. "Don't you?"

"I do," Bech admitted.

"It comes at you a little harder somehow. More *zap*. More subliminal leverage."

Bech nodded. This tall fellow for all his languor and rural costume talked Bech's language. They were in business.

BECH IS BACK! was to be the key of the advertising campaign. Newspaper ads, thirty-second radio spots, cardboard cutouts in the bookstores, posters showing Bech as of over a decade ago and Bech now. *Fifteen Years in the Making* was a subsidiary slogan. But first, nine months of gestation had to be endured, while proofs languished in the detention cells of book production and jacket designs wormed toward a minimum of bad taste. Back in Ossining, Bea was frantic over the loss of Ann's virginity. If only it had been Judy, she explained, she wouldn't be so shocked; but Ann had always been the good one, the A student, the heir to Rodney's seriousness.

"Maybe that's why," Bech offered. "It takes some seriousness to lose your virginity. Always flirting and hanging out with the cheerleaders like Judy, you get too savvy and the guys never lay a glove on you."

"Oh, what do you know? You've never had daughters."

"I had a sister," he said, hurt. "I had a twenty-one-year-old mistress once."

"I bet you did," Bea said. "Typical. You're just the kind of thing Rodney and I hoped would never happen to our girls."

The twins were seventeen. They would be eighteen on Valentine's Day. The deflowerer, if Judy could be believed, was one of the speckled crowd crunching around in the driveway with their fathers' cars. "I don't see that it's any big deal," Bech said. "I mean, it's a peer, it's puppy love, it's not rape or Charles Manson or anybody. Didn't I just read in a survey somewhere that the average American girl has had intercourse by around sixteen and a half?"

"That's with everybody figured in," Bea snapped. "The ghettos and Appalachia and all that. If I'd wanted my girls to be ghetto statistics I would have moved to a ghetto."

"Listen," Bech said, hurt again. "Some of my best ancestors grew up in a ghetto."

"Don't you *understand*?" Bea asked, her face white, her lips thinned. "It's a de*file*ment. A woman can never get it *back*."

"What would she do with it if she could get it back? Come on, sweetie. You're making too fucking much of this."

"Easy for you to say. Easy for you to say anything, evidently. Do you think this would have happened if that book of yours hadn't been in the house, all that crazy penthouse sex you cooked up out of your own sordid little flings?"

"I didn't know Ann had read it."

"She didn't have to. She heard us talking about it. It was in the air."

"Oh, please. It doesn't take a book of mine to put sex in the air."

"No of course not. Don't blame books for anything. They just sit there behind their authors' grins. You act as though the world is one thing and art is another and God forbid they should ever meet. Well, my daughter's virginity has been sacrificed, as I see it, to that damn dirty book of yours."

Bech had never seen Bea like this before, raging. What frightened him most were her eyes, unseeing, and the mouth that went on, a machine of medium-soft flesh that could not be shut off. This face that had nested in every fork of his body floated like some careening gull in the wind of her fury, staring red-rimmed at him as if to swoop at the exposed meat of his own face. "Jesus," he offered with mild exasperation. "The kid is seventeen. Let her fuck if that's what she wants."

"It's *not* what she wants, how could she want one of those awful boys? She *does*n't want it, that's the point; what she wants is to show *me*. Her mother. For leaving her father and screwing you."

"I thought it was Rodney who left."

"Oh, don't be so literal, you know how these things are. It takes two. But then my taking up with you, so quickly really, in that house on the Vineyard that time, and the way we've been here, so h-happy with each other"—her face was going from white to pink, and drifting closer to his—"I never thought of how it must look to them. The children. Especially the girls. Don't you see, I've made them face, what they shouldn't have had to face so early, their own mother's"—now her face was on his shoulder, her breath hot on his neck— "s-sexuality! And of *course* they hate it, of *course* they want to do self-destructive things out of spite!" He was in her grip, no less tight for her being grief-stricken. As her storm of remorse worked its way through Bea's fragile, Christian nervous system, tough, Semitic Bech, dreamer and doer both, author of the upcoming long-awaited *Think Big*, pondered open-eyed the knobbed and varnished and lightly charred mantel of their field-stone fireplace. Above it there was an oil painting, with a china-blue, single-clouded sky, of a clipper ship that Bea's maternal great-grandfather had once captained, depicted under full sail and cleaving a bottle-green sea as neatly crimped by waves as an old lady's perm; upon it, two phallic clay candlesticks, one by Ann and one by

Judy, executed by the twins in some vanished summer's art camp at Briarcliff and now by consecrated usage set on either end of the mantelpiece; beside it, a fishing rod with broken reel that Donald had chosen to lean forever in the corner where the fieldstones met the floral-wall-papered wall. Bourgeois life: its hooks came in all sizes.

He patted Bea's back and said, "And for all this you blame me?"

"Not you, *us*."

Like Adam and Eve. The first great romantic image, the Expulsion. The aboriginal trinity of producer, advertiser, and consumer. This woman's fair head was full of warping myths. Her sobbing had become its own delicious end, a debauchery of sorts, committed not with him but with Rodney's ghost, to the accompaniment of spiritual stride piano played by that honorary member of many a Jew-excluding organization, Judge R. Austin Latchett.

Tad slugs her. Bech looked around for cold water, and threw some. "What about birth control?" he asked.

Bea looked up out of her tear-mottled face. "What about it?"

"If the kid's humping, she better have it or you'll really have something to cry about."

Bea blinked. "Maybe it was only one time."

Bech flattened a tear at the side of her nose, tenderness returning. "I'm afraid it's not something you do only once. You get hooked. Have you ever talked to the girls about all this?"

"I suppose so," Bea said vaguely. "I know at school they took hygiene. . . . It's *hard*, Henry. For a long time they're so young it wouldn't make any sense and then suddenly they're so old you assume they must know it all and you'd feel foolish."

"Well, there're worse things than feeling foolish." It was hard for him, on his side, to believe that this woman needed his advice, his wisdom. The music of female mockery, and of its Southern cousin female adulation, had played in his ears for five decades; so it was hard for him to hear this shy wifely tune, this gentle halting request for guidance in a world little more transparent in its fundamental puzzles to female intuition than to male. "You must talk to her," Bech advised firmly.

"But how can I let her know I know anything without betraying Judy?"

The prototypical maze, Bech remembered reading somewhere, was the female insides. He tried to be patient. "You don't have to let her know. Just tell her as an item of general interest."

"Then I should be talking to them both at the same time."

She had a point there, he admitted to himself. Aloud he said, "No. In this area being a twin doesn't count anymore. You can imply to Ann you've had or will have the same conference with Judy, but for now you want to talk privately with *her*. Listen. The girl must know she's gotten in deep, she *wants* to hear from her mother. She's not going to grill you about what you know or how you know."

The more persuasively he talked, the more slack and dismayed her expression grew. "But what do I say ex-*act*ly, to start it off?"

"Say, 'Ann, you're reaching an age now when many girls in our society enter into sexual relations. I can't tell you I approve, because I don't; but there are certain medical options you should be aware of.' "

"It doesn't sound like me. She'll laugh."

"Let her. She's a little girl inside a woman's body. She's suddenly been given the power to make a new human life out of her own flesh. It's more frightening than getting a driver's license. She's more frightened than you are."

"How do you know so much?"

"I'm a man of the world. People are my profession."

A new thought struck Bea. "Don't boys like that use things?"

"Well, they used to, but in this day and age I expect they're too spoiled and lazy. They don't like that snappy feeling."

"But if I begin to talk contraception with her so calmly, it amounts to permission. I'm saying it's *fine*." Panic squeezed this last word out thin as a wire.

"Well, maybe it is fine," he said. "Think of Samoa. Of Zanzibar. Western bourgeois civilization, don't forget, is a momentary aberration in the history of *Homo sapiens*."

She heard the impatience of his tone, his boredom with wedded worry and wisdom. "Henry, I'm sorry. I'm being stupid. It's just I'm so scared of doing the wrong thing. For some reason I can't think."

"Well," he began in a deep voice, for the third time. "It's easy to give advice where it's not your own life and death. On the matter of my book, you were very hard-headed."

"And you resent it," she pointed out, dry-eyed at last.

Bech Wed

After this fraught discussion of sexuality, it seemed to Bech, Bea pulled back, she who had once been so giving and playful, so honestly charmed to find this new, hairier, older, more gnarled and experienced man in her bed. Now when at night, finished reading, he turned off his light and experimentally caressed her, she stiffened at his touch, for it interrupted her inner churning. Even under him and enclosing him, she felt absent. "What are you thinking about?" he would ask.

It would be as if he had startled her awake, though the whites of her eyes gleamed sleeplessly in the Ossining moonlight. Sometimes she would confess, blaming herself for both the girl's sin and this its frigid penance, "Ann."

"Can't you give it a rest?"

"God in Heaven I wish I could."

At Vellum, lanky laconic Flaggerty had a young female assistant, a quick black-haired girl fresh from Sarah Lawrence, and Bech wondered if it was her hands that showed in the Xeroxes the firm sent him of his galley sheets. Whoever it was had held each sheet flat on the face of the photocopier, and in the shadowy margins clear ghosts of female fingers showed, some so vivid a police department could have analyzed the fingerprints. Bech inspected these parts of disembodied hands with interest; they seemed smaller, slightly, than real hands, but then womanly smallness, capable of Belgian embroidery and Rumanian gymnastics, is one of the ways by which the grosser sex is captivated. He looked through the photocopied fingers for the hard little ghost of a wedding or engagement ring and found none; but then she might have been employing only her right hand.

At last Bea did take Ann aside, on an evening when Judy was working late on the senior yearbook, and they had their conversation. "It was just as you predicted," Bea told Bech in their bed. "She wasn't angry that I seemed to know, she seemed relieved. She cried in my arms, but she wouldn't promise to stop doing it. She isn't sure she loves the boy, but he's awfully sweet. We agreed I'd make an appointment with Doctor Landis to get her fitted for a diaphragm."

"Well then," he said. "After all that fuss."

"I'm sorry," Bea apologized. "I know I've been distracted lately. You want to make love now?"

"In principle," Bech said. "But in practice, I'm beat. Donald made me bowl six strings with him over at Pin Paradise and my whole shoulder aches. Also I thought I'd take the train into town tomorrow."

"Oh?"

"There're some things I want to go over on the galleys with Flaggerty. It's better if we can hash it out right there, and I want to be sharp. He's deceptive—all lazy and purring and next thing he's at your throat."

"I thought you said he never had any suggestions. Unlike that other editor you had years ago."

"Well, he didn't, but now he's developing some. I think he was babying me before, since I'm a living legend."

"O.K., dear. If you say so. Love you."

"Love you," Bech echoed, preparing to fold his mind into a dark shape, a paper airplane to be launched with a flick from the crumbling cliff of consciousness.

But Bea broke into his dissolution with the thought,

spoken aloud toward the ceiling, "I worry now about what Judy will say. Somehow I don't think she'll approve. She'll think I've been too soft."

His sweet suburban softy, Bech thought sibilantly, and slept.

At his suggestion next day Flaggerty introduced him to his assistant. "Arlene Schoenberg," Flaggerty said, stooping in his shirt of mattress ticking like some giant referee overseeing a jump-off between two opposing players at a midget basketball game. The girl was small, slender, and sleek, with hair in a Lady Dracula fall, a chin one centimeter longer than strictly necessary, and sable eyes fairly dancing, in their web of sticky lashes, with delight at meeting Henry Bech.

"Mr. Bech, I've admired you for *so* long—"

"I feel like old hat," Bech finished for her.

"Oh, *no*," the girl said, aghast.

"So you tote bales for Mr. Jim here," Bech said.

"Arlene has all the moves," Flaggerty said, shuffling, about to blow the whistle.

Bech had held on a half-second longer than necessary to her hand. Her dear small busy clever hand. It was much whiter than in the Xeroxes, and decidedly pulsing in his.

He glided back to Ossining as the early-winter dusk enwrapped the signal lights, the grudged wattage of the station platform, the vulnerable gold of the windows of homes burning in the distance, all softened by the tentative wet beginnings of a snowfall. His head and loins were light with possibility merely, for Flaggerty had taken him to lunch at a health-food restaurant where no liquor was served and, when they had returned, Arlene Schoenberg was absent on a crosstown errand. Bech drove his old Ford—only thirty-three thousand miles in eighteen years of ownership—home through the cosmic flutter. He was met by a wild wife. Bea pulled him into the downstairs bathroom so she could impart her terrible new news. "Now Judy wants one too!"

"One what?" Bea's eyes, after his brooding upon Arlene's dark, heavily lashed ones all through the lulling train ride, looked so bald and blue, Bech had to force himself to feel there was a soul behind this doll's stare.

"One *di*aphragm!" Bea answered, putting the lid hard on her desire to scream. "I asked her if she was making love to anybody and she said No and I told her they couldn't fit one in with her hymen intact and she said she broke hers horseback-riding years ago, and I just have no idea if she's lying or *not*. She was *aw*fully cocky, Henry; I know now I did the wrong thing with Ann, I *know* it." Bea uttered all this in a choked tearful rush; he had to hug her, there in the downstairs bathroom, the smallest room in the big house.

"You did the right thing," he had to say, for she had followed his advice.

"But why did Ann have to run right away and *tell* her?" Bea asked, betrayed.

"Bragging," Bech offered, already bored. He felt this woman's mind narrowing in like the vortex in a draining bathtub toward an obsession with her daughters' vaginas. There must be more to life than this. He asked Bea, "What would Rodney have done in this situation?"

It was the wrong name to invoke. "This situation wouldn't have *hap*pened if Rodney were still here," Bea said, making little fists and resting them on Bech's chest in lieu of thumping him.

"Really?" he asked, wondering whether this could be so. Rodney had gone from being a pill and a heel to become *in absentia* the very principle of order—the clockwork God of the Deists, hastily banished by the Romantic rebellion. "Could he really have stopped the girls from growing up?"

Bea's face was contorted and clouded by a rich pink veil of mourning for Rodney. Beyond a certain age, women are not enhanced by tears. Bech shrugged off her absent-minded grip upon him and snapped, "Here's a simple solution. Tell Judy she has to go out and get fucked first before you'll buy her a diaphragm."

Get a diaphragm the old-fashioned way, ran through his mind. *Earn it.* He left her weeping in the tiny room with its honorable solid turn-of-the-century plumbing and surveyed the weather from the bay windows. It was snowing hard now, thick as a ticker-tape parade. The mass of woods behind the house was toned down almost out of sight, and in the near foreground the spherical aluminum bird-feeder suspended from the old grape arbor swung softly back and forth like a bell buoy in a whispering white sea. Donald was outside trying to toboggan already on the fresh-fallen inch, and the twin girls were huddled giggling on the long orange sofa in the TV den, which had been intended a hundred years ago as a library. On its shelves Bech's books still waited to be integrated with the books already there. Rodney had been a history buff, and collected books on sailing. The girls' faces looked feverish with secrets. Their giggles stopped when Bech loomed in the doorway. "Why don't you two little angels," he asked them, "stop giving your mother a hard time with your nasty little cunts?"

"Fuck you, Uncle Henry," Judy managed to get out, though their four gray eyes stared in fright.

Rather than wax more ogreish, he climbed the stairs to his silver room and read proof for the hour before dinner. Mortimer Zenith, a minor character who took on an unexpected menace and dynamism in the third chapter, is outlining to poor fat, battered, snuffly, alcoholic Ginger Greenbaum the potential financial wonders of a divorce. Mortimer, too, has his designs on the lovely Olive, once he gets his own game show, which he is hoping Ginger will back, once she gets her share of Tad's money. Ginger, muddled and despairing though she is, cannot quite imagine life without Tad, whose scorn and long absences are somewhat mitigated by the afternoon consolations of Emilio, the young Filipino horsetrainer on their newly acquired Connecticut estate. What caught Bech's eye as he wrote, and now as he rewrote on proof, was the light at the great windows of the Greenbaum penthouse, while Mort and Ginger murmur and car horns—he crossed out "twinkle"—bleat ever more urgently ten stories below. The sky has sifted out of its harsh noon cobalt a kind of rosy brown banded behind the blackening profiles of the skyscrapers, here and there a cornice or gargoyle flaming in the dying light from the west. Rush hour, once again. Bech suddenly sees a pigeon alight on the sill outside, causing both scheming, curried heads to turn around simultaneously. At his own window, the outdoors was an opaque gray blanket. Individual pellets of snow ticked at the icy panes, like a tiny cry for help. Downstairs, a trio of female voices was lifted in pained chorus, chanting the scandal of Bech's brief exchange with the twins. The front door slammed as Donald came in frozen, his voice loud with complaint at the toboggan's performance. Happiness was up here, as the tendrils of emendation thickened along the margins and the electric heaters glazed Bech's shins with warmth. He glanced again at his window and was surprised not to see a pigeon there, with its cocked head and Chaplin-tramp style of walking, beady eye alert for a handout. *Tick. Tick.* Blizzards are ideal for doing proof, he thought. Socked in. Byrd at the South Pole. Raleigh in the Tower.

The storm felt sexy, but beneath the goosedown puff Bea whimpered to him, "I'm sorry, sweetie. This thing with the girls has exhausted me. Judy and Ann and I had a big cry about everything but it still all feels so up in the air." Wind softly whirred in the chimney of their bedroom fireplace, with its broken damper. Gently his hand sought to tug up the flannel of her nightie. "Oh, Henry, I just *can't*," Bea pleaded. "After all this upset I just feel *dirty* down there." When her breathing slowed to a sleeper's regularity, and the house sighed in all its walls as the storm cuffed its frame with rhythmic airy blows, Bech in his meteorological rapture masturbated, picturing instead of his own thick hand that small, dark, dirty Xeroxed one.

The snow descended for forty-eight hours, and they

were snowbound for another two days. The pack of pimply wolves attracted to this house by Ann and Judy's pheromones assembled now not in their fathers' cars but on cross-country skis and in one especially well equipped case on a Kawasaki snowmobile; the boys, puffed up by parkas to the size of that cheerful monster made out of Michelin tires, clumped in and out of the front hall, tracking snow and exhaling steam. Bea's immediate neighbors, too, tracked in and out, swapping canned goods and tales of frozen pipes and defrosted food lockers. The oral tradition in America was not quite dead, it seemed, as sagas of marooned cars, collapsed gazebos, and instant Alps beside the plowed parking lots downtown tumbled in. The worst privation in Ossining appeared to be the few days' non-delivery of *The New York Times*; withdrawal symptoms raged at breakfast tables and beset stolid bankers as they heaved at the snow in their driveways, recklessly aware of bubbles of ignorance in their bloodstreams that might reach their hearts. All day long, while feathers whipped from the spines of drifts and children dug tunnels and golden retrievers bounded up and down in the fluff like dolphins, people in hushed tones discussed the scandal of it, of being without the *Times*. Television stations flashed pictures of the front page, to reassure outlying districts that it was still being published, and the *Citizen Register* (serving Ossining, Briarcliff, Croton, Buchanan, Cortlandt) expanded its World/Nation section, but these measures only underlined the sense of dire emergency, of being cut off from all that was real. Bech retreated from the *Times*less hubbub to his silver-lined room, adding tendrils to his proofs like a toothpicked avocado pit sending down roots into a water glass. For the first time, he began to think he might really have something here. Maybe he really was back.

The gestation period of nine months dictated that *Think Big* be a summer book, and that helped it; it didn't have to slug it out with that musclebound autumnal crowd of definitive biographies or multi-generational novels with stark titles like *Lust* or *Delaware* and acknowledgment pages full of research assistants, nor with their hefty spring sisters, the female romancers and the feminist decriers of the private life. *Think Big* in its shiny aqua jacket joined the Popsicles and roller coasters, baseball games and beach picnics as one of that summer's larky things; "it melts in your mouth and leaves sand between your toes," wrote the reviewer for *The East Hampton Star*. "The squalid book we all deserve," said Alfred Kazin in *The New York Times Book Review*. "A beguilingly festive disaster," decreed John Leonard in the daily *Times*. "Not quite as *vieux chapeau* as I had every reason to fear," allowed Gore Vidal in *The New York Review of Books*. "Yet another occasion for rejoicing that one was born a woman," proclaimed Ellen Willis in *The Village Voice*. "An occasion for guarded wonder," boomed Benjamin De Mott in *Partisan Review*, "that puts us in grateful mind of Emerson's admonition, 'Books are the best of things, well used; abused, among the worst.'" "An occasion," proposed George Steiner in *The New Yorker*, "to marvel once again that not since the Periclean Greeks has there been a configuration of intellectual aptitude, spiritual breadth, and radical intuitional venturesomeness to rival that effulgence of middle-class, *Mittel*-European Jewry between, say, Sigmund Freud's first tentative experiments with hypnosis and Isaac Babel's tragic vanishing within Stalin's Siberian charnel houses."

People simply opined, "A blast, if you skip the scenery," and featured Bech and Bea repairing their grape arbor in his-and-hers carpenter coveralls. Even before the sparkling notices came rolling in, the fair-weather flags had been up. Bech was photographed by Jill Krementz, caricatured by David Levine, and interviewed by Michiko Kakutani. The Book-of-the-Month Club made *Think Big* its Alternate Alternate choice for July, with a Special Warning to Squeamish Subscribers. Bantam and Pocket Books engaged in a furious bidding of which the outcome was a well-publicized figure with more zeroes than a hand has fingers. "Bech Is *In!*" *Vogue* splashed in a diagonal banner across a picture of him modelling a corduroy coat and a ribbed wool turtleneck. "Bech Surprises" was *Time*'s laconic admission in a belated follow-up piece, they having ignored *Think Big* during publication week in favor of a round-up of diet cook books. What surprised Bech, that remarkably fair summer, was seeing his book being read, at beaches and swimming pools, by lightly toasted teen-agers and deep-fried matrons and even by a few of his male fellow commuters during his increasingly frequent trips to New York. To think that those shuttling eyes were consuming the delicate, febrile interplay of Tad and Thelma, or of Olive and Mort, or of Ginger and her Filipino while lilacs droopy with bloom leaned in at the open upper half of the stable door and the smell of oats mingled with human musk—the thought of it embarrassed Bech; he wanted to pluck the book from its readers' hands and explain that these were only his idle dreams, hatched while captive in Sing Sing, unworthy of their time let alone their money.

Having taken Donald swimming one day at the pool of Bea and Rodney's old club, Bech saw a bronze and zaftig young woman on a plastic-strap chaise holding the book up against the sun, reading it through her rhinestone-studded sunglasses. "How's it going?" he asked aloud, feeling guilty at the pain he must be giving her—the squint, the ache in her upholding arm. She lowered the book and stared at him, dazed and annoyed; it was as if he had awakened her. He saw from the tightening of her zinc-white lips that she made no connection between the world she had been immersed in and this stocky, woolly male intruder in outmoded plaid trunks, and that if he did not instantly move away she would call for the life-guard. Yet she had an appealing figure, and must have an emptiness within, which his book was in some sense fill-ing. He was his own rival. He came to flinch at the sight of his aqua jackets; they were as vivid to his sensitized sight as swimming pools seen from an airplane. He had filled the world with little distorting mirrors. *Think Big* was in its sixth printing by September, and Big Billy telegraphed in congratulation from Hawaii, GROW OLD ALONG WITH ME THE BEST IS YET TO COME.

He couldn't even take Arlene Schoenberg to lunch in an unprestigious Italian restaurant without some nitwit asking him to sign a scrap of paper—usually one of those invitations to a "health club" staffing topless masseuses that are handed out all over sordid midtown. Every time an autograph-seeker approached, it put more stardust in Arlene's eyes and set seduction at another remove. The world, by one of those economic balancings whereby it steers, had at the same time given him success and taken from him the writer's chief asset, his privacy. Her little fascinating hands enticingly fiddled with her knife and fork, caressed her Campari-and-soda, and dropped to her lap. After a moment, like an actress taking a curtain call, one of them returned into sight to scratch with a fingernail at an invisible itch on the side of her slightly long chin. She asked him where he got his ideas, from real life or out of his imagination. She asked him if he thought a writer owed anything to society or just to himself. She asked him if he had always been such a neat typist and good speller; now, her little brothers and sisters, none of them could spell, it was really shocking, you wonder if there will be any books at all in twenty years, the terrible way it's going. Bech told her that credit for his typing and spelling should go to Mae, a dark genius his wife had found for him in Ossining. In an attempt to steer Miss Schoenberg's fascination away from his professional self, he talked a good deal about his wife. He gave Bea credit for finally settling him down in front of a type-writer and getting him to finish his book. He further confessed, putting the intimacy level up a notch, that when he had married her he had not realized what a worrier she was: she had seemed, in contrast to her diffi-cult sister, Norma, so calm and understanding, so, well, motherly. And indeed she had proved motherly: she thought about her kids all the time, and nearly went wild when one of her daughters began to—Bech hesitated, for this starstruck minx was also somebody's daughter, and the word "fuck" or "screw," running ahead as a kind of scout, might startle her into a defensive posture— "misbehave," he said. As he spoke, the house in Ossining, with its dome-shaped lawn and coarse green exoskeleton and cool silver-lined retreat, became uncomfortably real. The storm windows were only half up. Some insulation needed to be taped and restapled in his study. Bech wondered if the magic appeal of those Xeroxed hands, haunting the edges of his duplicated galleys, might not have been a mirage peculiar to that cloistered environment. Certainly Miss Schoenberg, as she sat perkily across from him in her sparrow-colored sweater, gave signs of being common.

"It must be terribly exciting to be a writer's wife," she said. "I mean, she must never know what you're thinking."

"Oh, I expect she knows as much as she wants to."

"I mean, when you look at her, she must feel she's being X-rayed. You write about women so well, she must feel naked."

Campari-and-soda always gave Bech the same sensation as swallowing aspirin: that burny feeling at the top of the esophagus. Thinking of naked, he stared glumly at Arlene's thready sweater and found it utterly opaque. Did she have breasts in there, or typewriter spools? She was wearing a thin gold chain which nobody had ripped off her neck yet. And she was going on, "Writers have such rich fantasy lives, I think that's what makes them so fascinating to women."

"Richer, you think, than, say, Mr. Flaggerty's fantasy life?"

It was an inspired stab. She said petulantly, "Oh *him*, all he fantasizes about is the Mets and then the Jets. Really. And where to get good Mexican brown like they used to groove on at college when he was picketing the ROTC and marching with Dylan and all that."

"You seem," Bech ventured, "to know him pretty well."

For the first time, her eyes lost their starry celebrity shine and submitted to an amused and sexual narrowing. "Well enough. He's a good boss. I've had worse."

Bech nostalgically wished he were back home raking the lawn. But Arlene Schoenberg was just getting relaxed, her shapely hands deftly twirling green fettucini onto a fork. The restaurant skills of New York women: like praying mantises roving the twigs of a creosote bush. He should have had more Gothamesque eating-out in his book. And the way the tables are moving out into the streets, into the soot. His silence brought a slow smile to Arlene's face, showing a provocative rim of gum. "See," she said. "I have no idea what you're thinking."

"I was wondering," he told her, "if there was a way we could get Vellum to pay for this lunch. Can you forge Flaggerty's signature, or aren't you that friendly yet?"

Her eyes became solemn bright circles again. "Oh, no."

"O.K., then. On me. What else can I do for you?"

"Well"—she absent-mindedly, tuggingly fiddled up a loop into her gold chain and squeezed her finger in it so that the tip turned bright red—"that brother I was telling you about, you know, *did* want me to ask you if you could possibly come talk to his seventh-grade class, it's a special school for dyslexics out toward Glen Cove, they'd be *so*, you know—"

Bech saw his opportunity and took it. He patted her bare hand as it lay distracted on the checked tablecloth. "I'd like to," he told her, "but I can't. The last time I spoke in a school I got involved in a disastrous affair with a woman who only cared about the literary me. She spurned the man. Wasn't that rotten of her?"

"I'd have to know the circumstances," Arlene Schoenberg prudently said, as if there had never been a sexual revolution, and pulled back her hand to cope further with the fettucini.

On the walk from the restaurant back to the Vellum offices, they passed the Doubleday window, which held a pyramid of *Think Big*s. Bech always pitied his books, seen in a bookstore; they looked so outnumbered. He had sent them forth to fight in inadequate armor, with guns that jammed. These unbought copies were beginning to fade and warp in the daily slant of sun. On the train home, he saw how many of the yellowing trees were already bare. Soon it would be a year since he had finished the book Bea had got him to sit down and write. Their household had changed: the girls were off at college, Ann at M.I.T. and Judy at Duke, and little Donald no longer wanted his stepdad to take him places. Each fall they used to go to one Ossining High School football game together, played by mostly black players on a field where you could smell the torn earth and hear each cheerleader's piping voice fragile against the sky. This year the boy, newly thirteen, had looked disdainful and begged off. His father's snobbery was welling up through his genes. Rodney had taken Donald instead to the Harvard-Princeton game, at Palmer Stadium.

The house crackled in its timbers and joints, now that the furnace was on again and a heat differential applied torque. Workmen were busy inside the house and out; since Bech's book had made a million dollars, the north face of the mansard roof was being given new slates and the grand front staircase was being fully refinished, after ten years of a half-scraped left-hand banister. The television crew of *Sixty Minutes* had come and rearranged all the furniture, exposing how shabby it was. Within the many rooms Bech had been somewhat avoiding Bea; she wanted mostly to talk about their household expenditures, or to complain that Donald kept climbing on the roofers' scaffolding after they had gone for the day. "He has these horrible new delinquent friends, Henry. With Ann and Judy off I thought we'd be so relaxed now."

"How did that ever work out, by the way, with the diaphragms?"

She looked blank. If there was one thing Bech resented about women, it was the way they so rapidly forgave themselves for the hysteria they inflicted on others. He prompted, "You remember, Judy wanted one too, but she was still a virgin. . . ."

"Oh. Yes. Didn't I tell you? It was very simple, I don't know why we didn't think of it. Doctor Landis fitted Ann for one, and then gave me a prescription for two the same size. After all, they *are* twins."

"Brilliant," Bech sighed.

"Sweetie, could you spare a minute and look at these Sloane's catalogues with me? What I'd like to do around the fireplace is get sort of a conversation-pit feeling without having it look like a ski lodge. Do you think boxy modern looks silly on a big Oriental?"

The hinges of his jaw ached with a suppressed yawn. "I think," he said, "the room looks nice enough now."

"You're not focusing. The staircase being all new and shiny shows everything else up. If it's the cost you're worried about, Sheila Warburton says with things so unsettled in the Middle East *any* Oriental you buy is a better investment than stocks, than gold—"

"I love those old wing chairs," Bech said. In the evenings he would sit in one, his feet up on an inverted bushel basket that was meant to hold wood, and read; he was reading Thomas Mann on Goethe, Wagner, Nietzsche, Schopenhauer, and Freud these nights. What chums they all turned out to have been!

"Those chairs were Rodney's mother's, and he really should have them back now that he has a bigger apartment."

"Bea, you know we don't *have* the million dollars yet, it's just a bunch of bits in Vellum's computer. I won't get my first royalties till next August."

"That was another thing Sheila Warburton said: you were crazy not to ask for a whopping advance, with inflation the way it is."

"*Damn* Sheila Warburton, and that pompous Paul as well. Nobody knew the book would take off like this. In the old days a respectable author *nev*er asked for an advance; that was strictly for the no-talents starving down in the Village."

Standing contemplative in her room of imagined furniture, Bea was hard to rattle. She slowly woke to his tone of indignation and came and embraced him. She had been raking leaves in an unravelling ski sweater that smelled muskily of leafmold and lank autumn grass. "But these aren't the old days, Henry," she said, tickling his ear with her breath. "It costs a fortune to live down in the Village now. And you aren't the old Henry, either." She shuddered in happiness, and in her spasm gave him a squeeze. "We're all so *proud* of you!"

If there was another thing Bech resented about women it was the way they enveloped—the way they yearned, at moments of their convenience, to dissolve the sanitary partition between I and Thou. Assimilation, the most insidious form of conquest. He was becoming a shred of leafmold. "I don't know about that book," he began.

"The book is wonderful," she interrupted, with breathy impatience. "When do we do another?"

"Another?" The thought sickened him. A whole new set of names to invent, a theme to nurture within like a tumor, a texture to maintain page after page . . . His suburban softy, his plot of earth, was insatiable.

"Sure," Bea said briskly, backing off. "The storm windows are up, you've done all the publicity the media can stand, you've said the same things to twenty different interviewers, what are you going to do with your days?"

"Well, there've been some invitations to read at colleges. Some little agricultural college in West Virginia sounded interesting, and an Indian school in South Dakota—"

"Oh you've *done* all that," Bea said. "You don't need to go expose yourself for peanuts anymore, or fuck those little coeds in the Ramada Inn. Don't think I don't know really why you did all that speaking." Her sideways glance was both hostile and flirtatious, a common marital combination.

And he resented female knowingness, its coy invasion, its installation of an *Oberführer* in every province of his person. His mind, body, mouth, genitals—Bea had possessed them all and set up checkpoints along every escape route. His "triumph" (to quote *Vogue* again) was more deeply hers than his; that night in bed, when she insisted on copulating, it was, he felt, with the body of her own triumphant wifeliness that she came to climax, cooing above him and then breaking into that ascending series of little yips that had the effect, on this occasion at least, of swallowing up his own climax as something relatively trivial. More and more Bea favored the female-superior position. As the air in the bedroom seasonally cooled, she kept on her nightie, becoming in the dark a tent of chiffon and lace and loose blond hair, an operatic apparition whose damp grip upon him was swaddled and unseen as she pulled him up forcefully into manhood, into

: 169 :

achievement, into riches and renewed fame, into viscid fireworks and neural release. She collapsed onto his chest panting.

"I feel so satisfied with you," she confided.

"And I with you," he responded, trusting the formal grammar to shade his inevitable and as it were pre-shaped rejoinder.

She heard the shadow. "Aren't you pleased?" she asked. "Not only about the book but about *us*? Tell me."

"Yes, I'm pleased. Of course."

"You were such a sad person then, Henry." Then. Before their marriage had infiltrated every cell and extracted daily wordage and nightly semen.

"I was?"

"*I* thought so," Bea said. "You used to frighten me. Not just sad. Other things, too. A lovely man, but, I don't know, sterile. You're so sweet with Donald."

Her arm across his chest was wonderfully heavy. He felt pegged down, and the image of Donald was another luminous nail. "We get along," he admitted. "But the kid's growing up."

Bea would not allow even so faint a discord to be the final note. "He loves you," she uttered, and as she slept he could see by moonlight that a smile remained on her face, rounding the cheek not buried in the pillow.

In his dream he is free. The landscape seems European —low gray sky, intense green fields, mud underfoot, churned and marked by tire treads and military boots. He has escaped from somewhere; fear is mixed sourly with his guilt, guilt at having left all those others behind, still captive. Yet in the meantime there are the urgencies of escape to cope with: dogs pursuing him are barking, and a hedge offers a place to hide. He squeezes in, his heart enormous and thumping. Candy wrappers litter the ground underfoot. The hedge is too wintry and thin; he will be discovered. In that thick gray European wool overhead, a single unseen bomber drones. It is, he instinctively knows, his only hope, though it will bring destruction. He awakes, and recognizes the drone as the furnace floors below. The neighborhood dogs have been harrying something, a raccoon perhaps, and downstairs Max had sleepily joined in with a gruff bark or two. Yet terror and guilt were slow to drain from Bech's system.

That afternoon, Bea had to pick up Donald after school and take him to the orthodontist and then to buy some school clothes; he had outgrown last year's. The child's smile had sprouted touching silver bands, and the first few pimples, harbingers of messy manhood, marred the skin that had once seemed perfect. They would not be home until six at the earliest. Bech roamed the great house with a vague sense of having lost something, a Minotaur restless in his maze. Around four, the doorbell rang. He expected to open it upon a UPS deliveryman or one of Bea's Ossining sipping companions; but the woman on the porch was Bea's sister, Norma Latchett.

Where middle age had brought out Bea's plumpness, it had whittled Norma down, making her appear even more stringy, edgy, and exasperated than formerly. Her dark hair was turning gray and she was not dyeing it but pulling it back from her brow severely. Yet her black wool suit was smart, her lipstick and eye shadow were this fall's correct shade and amount, and across her face, when it proved to be he who opened the door, flickered all the emotions of a woman first alarmed by and then measuring up to judgment by a former lover. "Where's Bea?" she asked.

Bech explained, and invited her in to wait until six or so.

Norma hesitated, clutching her pocketbook and looking slightly too trim, like the Avon lady. "I'm heading north to give a talk in Poughkeepsie and thought I'd say hello. Also I have some papers for Bea to sign. You two never come to the city anymore."

"Bea hates it," Bech said. "What are you giving your talk about? Come in, for heaven's sake. Just me and Max are here, and we aren't biting today."

"Oh, the usual thing," Norma said, looking vexed but entering the great varnished foyer. Since the workmen had done the refinishing it gleamed like the cabin of a yacht. "Those awful icons." For years, Norma had held jobs off and on in museums, and in these last ten years, as hope of marriage faded, had put herself seriously to school, and become an expert on Byzantine and Russian Orthodox art. Icons becoming ever more "collectible," she included bankers as well as students in the audience for her expertise. She lit a cigarette whose paper was tinted pale green, and looked switchily about for an ash-tray.

"Let's go into the living room," Bech said. "I'll build a fire."

"You don't have to entertain me, I could push on to Vassar and make the art department chairman give me dinner. Except I hate to eat before I talk, the blood all rushes to your stomach and makes you very stupid."

"I don't think anything could make you *very* stupid," he said gallantly, remembering as he followed her in past the pompous staircase how her body had concealed surprising amplitudes—her hips, for instance, were wide, as if the pelvic bones had been spread by a childbirth that had never occurred, and so that her thighs scarcely touched, giving her a touching knock-kneed look, naked or in a bathing suit. He took three of the logs he had split last winter in hopes that the exercise would prolong his life, and laid a fire while she settled into one of the wing chairs, his favorite, the one covered in maroon brocade, that he usually read in. The match flared. The crumpled *Times* caught. The pine kindling began to crackle. He stood up, asking, "Tea?" His heart was thumping, as in last night's dream. The house in all its rooms held silent around them like the eye of a storm. Max padded in, claws clicking, and dropped himself with a ponderous sigh on the rug before the quickening flames. One golden eye with a red lower lid questioned Bech before closing. "Or a real drink?" Bech pursued. "I'm not sure we have white crème de menthe. Bea and I don't drink that much." Norma had, he remembered, a fondness for vodka stingers, for Black Russians, for anything whose ingredients one was likely not to have.

"I never drink before I talk," she said sharply. "I'm wondering, if I'm going to stay, if I should bring my slides in from the car. You leave them in a cold car too long, they sometimes crack in the heat of the projector."

As Bech retrieved the gray metal box from the trunk
of her car, Max trotted along with him, letting one of
Norma's tires have his autograph and running a quick
check on the woodchuck trying to hibernate underneath
the porch. In returning, Bech closed the front door on
the dog's rumpled, affronted face. Three's a crowd.

The slides tucked safely beneath her chair, beside her
outsize alligator purse, Norma asked, "Well. How does it
feel?"

"How does what feel?" This time her cigarette was
violet in tint. They must come mixed in the box, like
gumdrops.

"Having pulled it off."

"What off?" The nylon sheen of her ankles picked up
an orange glimmer from the fireplace flames; her eyes
held wet and angry sparks.

"Don't play dumb," she said. "That book. She got you
to make a million. Busy Bea, buzz, buzz."

"She didn't get me to do anything, it just happened. Is
happening. They say there's going to be a movie. Sure
you don't want any tea?"

"Stop being grotesque. Sit down. I have your chair."

"How can you tell?"

"The look on your face when I sat here. It didn't just
happen, she's bragging all the time about how she got
you your little *room*, and told you to write a few pages
every *day*, and keep going no matter how *rot*ten it was,
and how now the money's rolling in. How does it feel,
being a sow's ear somebody's turned into a silk purse?"

He had thought they might trade a few jabs with the
big gloves on; but this was a real knife fight. Norma was

furious. The very bones in her ankles seemed to gnash as she crossed and recrossed her legs. "Did you read the book?" Bech mildly asked her.

"As much as I could. It's lousy, Henry. The old you would never have let it be published. It's slapdash, it's sentimental, it's *cozy*. That's what I couldn't forgive, the coziness. Look how everybody loves it. You know that's a terrible sign."

"Mm," he said, a syllable pressed from him like a whistle from the chimney, like a creak from the house.

"I don't blame you; I blame Bea. It was she who forced it out of you, she and her cozy idea of marriage, to make a monument to herself. What if the monument *was* made of the bodies of all your old girl friends, *she's* the presiding spirit, she's the one who reaps the profit. Top dog. Bea always had to be top dog. You should have seen her play tennis, before she got so fat." Norma's eyes blazed. The demons of vengeance and truth had entered this woman, a dazzling sight.

"Bodies of old girl friends—?" Bech hesitantly prompted.

"Christ, Henry, it was a pyre. Smoke rising to heaven, to the glory of big fat Bea. Thanks by the way for calling me Thelma, so all my friends can be sure it's me."

"Thelma wasn't exactly . . ." he began. And, thinking of Bea herself, her soft body in bed, the way her eyelids and nose looked rubbed and pink when she was sad or cold, he knew that the rebirth and growth of *Think Big* weren't quite as Norma had described them, making something sudden and crass out of all those patient months spent tapping away amid the treetops and the flying squirrels. Still, she put the book in a fresh harsh light, and a fresh light is always liberating. "Bea *is* pleased about the money," he admitted. "She wants to refurnish the entire house."

"You bet she does," Norma said. "You should have seen the way she took over the dollhouse my parents had meant for both of us. She's greedy, Henry, and materialistic, and small-minded. Why does she keep you out here with these ridiculous commuters? The real question is, Why do you permit it? You've always been weak, but weak in your own way before, not in somebody else's. I guess I better have tea after all. To shut me up." She pinched her long lips tight to dramatize and turned her head so her profile looked pre-Raphaelite against the firelight. Some strands of her hair had strayed from severity, as if a light wind were blowing.

He perched forward on the lemon-colored wing chair and asked, "Didn't you at least like the part where Mort Zenith finally gets Olive alone in the beach cabaña?"

"It was cranked out, Henry. Even where it was good, it felt cranked out. But don't mind me. I'm just an old discarded mistress. You've got Prescott and Cavett with you and they're the ones that count."

In the barny old kitchen, its butcher-block countertops warping and its hanging copper pans needing Brillo, the tea water took forever to boil: Bech was burning to get back to his treasure of truth, arrived like an arrow in Ossining. He was trembling. Dusk was settling in outside. Max woofed monotonously at the back door, where he was usually at this hour let in and fed. When Bech returned with the two steaming cups and a saucer of Ritz crackers to the living room, Norma stood up. Her wool suit wore a fuzzy corona; her face in shadow loomed featureless. He set the tray down carefully on the inverted bushel basket and, giving the response that seemed expected, held and kissed her. Her mouth was wider and wetter than Bea's and, by virtue of longer acquaintance, more familiar. "I have a question for you," he said. "Do you ever fuck before you talk?"

They were so careful. They let Max in and closed the kitchen door. Upstairs, they chose Donald's bed because, never made, it would not show mussing. The boy's shelves still held the stuffed toys and mechanical games of childhood. A tacked-up map of the world, in the projection that looks like a flattened orange peel, filled Bech's vision with its muted pinks and blues when his eyelids furtively opened. *So this is adultery*, he thought: this homely, friendly socketing. An experience he would have missed, but for marriage. A sacred experience, like not honoring your father and mother. Good old Norma, she still had a faintly sandy texture to her buttocks and still liked to have her nipples endlessly, endlessly flicked by the attendant's tongue. She came silently, even sullenly, without any of Bea's angelic coos and yips. They kept careful track of the time by the clown-faced plastic clock on Donald's maple dresser, and by five-thirty Bech was downstairs pouring Kibbles into Max's bowl. The dog ate greedily, but would never forgive him. Bech cleared away the telltale untasted tea, washed and dried the cups, and put them back on their hooks. What else? Norma herself, whom he had last seen wandering in insouciant nudity toward the twins' bathroom for a shower, was maddeningly slow to get dressed and come back downstairs; he wanted her desperately to go, to disappear, even forever. But she had brought in her big reptilian pocketbook some documents connected with old Judge Latchett's estate—the release of some unprofitable mutual-fund shares—that needed Bea's signature. So they waited together in the two wing chairs. Bech took the maroon this time. Max went and curled up by the front door, pointedly. Norma cleared her throat and said, "I *did*, actually, like that bit with Zenith and your heroine. Really, it has a lot of lovely things in it. It's just I hate to see you turn into one more scribbler. Your paralysis was so beautiful. It was . . . statuesque."

Her conceding this, in softened tones, had the effect of making her seem pathetic. A mere woman, skinny and aging, hunched in a chair, his seed and sweat showered from her. In praising his book even weakly she had shed her dark magic. Bad news had been Norma's beauty. She was getting nervous about the talk she had to give. "If they aren't back by six-fifteen, I really *will* have to leave."

But Donald and Bea returned at six-ten, bustling in the door with crackling packages while the dog leaped to lick their faces. Donald's face had that stretched look of being brave; he had been told he must keep wearing retainers for two more years. Bea was of course surprised to find her sister and her husband sitting so primly on either side of a dying fire. "Didn't Henry at least offer you a drink?"

"I didn't want any. It might make me need to pee in the middle of my lecture."

"You poor thing," Bea said. "I'd be impossibly nervous." She knew. Somehow, whether by the stagy purity of their waiting or the expression of Max's ears or simple Latchett telepathy, she knew. Bea's blue eyes flicked past Bech's face like a piece of fair sky glimpsed between tunnels high in the mountains. And little Donald, he knew too, looking from one to the other of them with a wary brightness, feeling this entire solid house suspended above him on threads no more substantial than the invisible currents between these tall adults.

White on White

No sooner had the great success of *Think Big* sunk into the general social consciousness along the upper East Side than engraved invitations had begun to arrive at the Bechs' Ossining house. After Bech moved out, Bea in her scrupulous blue handwriting would forward these creamy stiff envelopes, including those addressed to "Mr. and Mrs.," to Bech's two drab sublet rooms on West Seventy-second Street. (Bech had taken these rooms in haste, renting from a disreputable friend of Flaggerty's, and though he deplored the tattered old acid-trip decor—straw mats, fringed hassocks—he was surprised by how much better he slept here than in bucolic splendor, surrounded by cubic yards of creaking, solid-black space for whose repair and upkeep he had become at least half responsible.) Many of his invitations he dropped into the plastic wastebasket, after lovingly thumbing them as examples of the engraver's art and the stationer's trade; but he tended to accept those that carried with them the merest lint or stray thread of old personal connection. His marriage having dissolved around him like the airy walls of a completed novel, anyone who knew Bech "when" interested him, as a clue to his past and hence to his future.

Mr. and Mrs. Henderson Hyde, III
and
Colortron Photographics, Inc.
request the pleasure of your company
at a party, honouring the publication of

White on White

by Angus Desmouches, esquire
on Friday, the thirteenth of April
at six o'clock

R.s.v.p.
124-7777

Suggested dress
All white

Bech remembered being photographed by the young and eager Angus Desmouches for *Flair*, long defunct, in the mid-Fifties, when *Travel Light* was coming out, to a trifling stir. The youthful photographer had himself looked at first sight as if seen through a wide-angle lens, his broad, tan, somehow Aztec face and wide head of wiry black hair dwindling to a pinched waist and tiny, tireless feet; clicking and clucking, he had pursued Bech up and down the vales and bike paths of Prospect Park, and then for contrast had taken him by subway to lower Manhattan and posed him stony-faced among granite skyscrapers. Bech had scarcely been back to the financial district in the decades since, though now he had a lawyer there, who, with much well-reimbursed head-wagging, was trying to disentangle him and his recent financial gains from Bea and her own tough crew of head-waggers. In a little bookshop huddled low in the gloom of Wall Street Bech had flipped through a smudged display copy of *White on White* ($128.50 before Christmas, $150 thereafter): finely focused platinum prints of a cigarette butt on a plain white saucer, a white kitten on a polar-bear rug, an egg amid feathers, a naked female foot on a tumbled bedsheet, a lump of sugar held in bared teeth, a gob of what might be semen on the margin of a book, a white-hot iron plunged into snow.

Bech went to the party. The butler at the door of the apartment looked like a dancer in one of the old M-G-M musical extravaganzas, in his white tie, creamy tails, and wing collar. The walls beyond him had been draped in bleached muslin; the apartment's regular furniture had been replaced with white wicker and with great sailcloth pillows; boughs and dried flowers spray-painted white had been substituted for green plants; most remarkably, in the area of the duplex where the ceiling formed a dome twenty feet high, a chalky piano and harp shared a platform with a tall vertical tank full of fluttering, ogling albino tropical fish. Angus Desmouches bustled forward, seemingly little changed—the same brown pug face and gladsome homosexual energy—except that his crown of black hair, sticking out stiff as if impregnated with dry-

ing paste, had gone stark white. So stark Bech guessed it
had been dyed rather than aged that color; his eyebrows
matched, it was too perfect. The years had piled celebrity and wealth upon the little photographer but not
added an inch to his waist. He looked resplendent in a
satin plantation suit. Bech felt dowdy in an off-white
linen jacket, white Levi's, and tennis shoes he had made a
separate trip out to Ossining to retrieve.

"Gad, it's good to press your flesh," Desmouches exclaimed, seeming in every cubic centimeter of his own
flesh to mean it. "How long ago was that, anyway?"

"Nineteen fifty-five," Bech said. "Not even twenty-
five years ago. Just yesterday."

"You were such a sweet subject, I remember that. So
patient and funny and wise. I got some delicious angles
on especially the downtown take, but the foolish, *fool*ish
magazine didn't use any of it, they just ran a boring head-
and-shoulders under some weeping *wil*low. I've always
been afraid you blamed *me*."

"No blame," Bech said. "Absolutely no blame in
this business. Speaking of which, that's some book of
yours."

The other man's miniature but muscular hands fluttered skyward in simultaneous supplication and dis-
avowal. "The idea came to me when I dropped an aspirin
in the bathtub and couldn't find it for the longest time.
The idea, you know, of exploring how little contrast you
could have and still have a photograph." His hands
pressed as if at a pane of glass beside him. "Of taking
something to the *li*mit."

"You did it," Bech told the air, for Desmouches like

: 183 :

a scarf up a magician's sleeve had been whisked away, to greet other guests in this white-on-white shuffle. Bech was sorry he had come. The house in Ossining had been empty, Donald off at school and Bea off at her new job, being a part-time church secretary under some steeple up toward Brewster. Max had been there, curled up on the cold front porch, and had wrapped his mouth around Bech's hand and tried to drag him in the front door. The door was locked, and Bech no longer had a key. He knew how to get in through the cellar bulkhead, past the smelly oil tanks. The house, empty, seemed an immense, vulnerable shell, a *Titanic* throttled down to delay its rendezvous with the iceberg. Its emptiness did not, oddly, much welcome him. In the brainlessly short memories of these chairs and askew rugs he was already forgotten; minute changes on all sides testified to his absence. Bea's clothes hung in her closet like cool cloth knives seen on edge, and in the way his remaining shoes and his tennis racket had been left tumbled on the floor of his own closet he read a touch of disdain. He turned up the thermostat a degree, lest the pipes freeze, before sneaking back out through the cellar and walking the two miles to the train station, through the slanting downtown, where he had always felt like a strolling minstrel.

The drinks served at this party were not white, nor was the bartender. An ebony hand passed him the golden bourbon. The host and hostess came and briefly cooed their pleasure at Bech's company. Henderson Hyde may have been a third but he came from some gritty town in the Midwest and had the ebullient urbanity of those who have wrapped themselves in Manhattan as in a sumptuous cloak. His wife, too, was the third—a former model whose prized slenderness was with age becoming gaunt. Her great lipglossed smile stretched too many tendons in her neck; designer dresses hung on her a trifle awkwardly, now that they were truly hers; her tenure as wife had reached the expensive stage. Tonight's gown, composed of innumerable crescent slices as of quartz, suggested the robe of an ice-maiden helper that Santa had taken on while rosy-cheeked Mrs. Claus looked the other way. Until he had married Bea, Bech had imagined that Whitsuntide had something to do with Christmas. Not at all, it turned out. And there was an entire week called Holy Week, corresponding to the seven days of Pesach. They were in it, actually.

"Smash of a book," said Hyde, giving the flesh above Bech's elbow a comradely squeeze as expertly as a doctor taps the nerves below your kneecap.

"You got through it?" Bech asked, startled. His funny bone tingled.

Mrs. Hyde intervened. "I told him all about it," she said. "He couldn't get to sleep for all my chuckling beside him as I read it. That scene with the cameramen!"

"It's top of the list I'm going to get to on the Island this summer. Christ, the books keep piling up," Hyde snarled. He was wearing, Bech only now noticed in the sea of white, a brilliant bulky turban and a caftan embroidered with the logo of his network.

"It's hard to read anything," Bech admitted, "if you're gainfully employed."

Somebody had begun to tinkle the piano: "The White Cliffs of Dover." *There'll be bluebirds over . . .*

"So sorry your wife couldn't be with us," Hyde's wife said in parting.

"Yeah, well," Bech said, not wanting to explain, and expecting they knew enough anyway. "Easy come, easy go." He had meant this to be soothing, but an alarmed look flitted across Mrs. Hyde III's gracious but overelastic features.

The harp joined in, and the melody became "White Christmas." *Just like the ones we used to know* . . . A man of his acquaintance, a fellow writer, the liberal thinker Maurie Leonard, came up to him. Maurie, though tall, and thick through the shoulders and chest, had such terrible, deskbound posture that all effect of force was limited to his voice, which emerged as an urgent rasp. Metal on metal. Mind on matter. "Some digs, huh?" he said. "You know how Hyde made his money, don'tcha?" More than a liberal, a radical whose twice-weekly columns were deplored by elected officials and whose bound essays were removed from the shelves of public-school libraries, Maurie yet took an innocent prideful glee in the awful workings of capitalism.

"No. How?" Bech asked.

"Game shows!" Maurie ground the words out through a mirth that pressed his cheeks up tight against his eyes, whose sockets were as wrinkled as walnuts. *Hyde-Jinks*, *Hyde-'n'-seek*. Haven't you heard of 'em? Christ, you just wrote a whole book about the TV industry!"

"That was fiction," Bech said.

Maurie, too, exerted pressure on the flesh above Bech's elbow, muttering confidentially, "You wouldn't know it to look at the uptight little prick, but Hyde's a genius.

He's like Hitler—the worst thing you can think of, he's there ahead of you already. Know what his latest gimmick is?"

"No," Bech said, beginning to wish that this passage were not in dialogue but in simple expository form.

"Mud wrestling!" Maurie rasped, and a dozen wrinkles fanned upward from each outer corner of his Tartarish, street-wise eyes. "In bikinis, right there on the boob tube. Not your usual hookers, either, but the girl next door; they come on the show with their husbands and mothers and goddamn gym teachers and talk about how they want to win for the hometown and Jesus and the American Legion and the next thing you see there they are, slugging another bimbo with a fistful of mud and taking a bite out of her ass. Christ, it's wonderful. One or two falls and they could be fucking stark naked. Wednesdays at five-thirty, just before the news, and then reruns Saturday midnight, for couples in bed. Bech, I defy you to watch without getting a hard-on."

This man loves America, Bech thought to himself, *and he writes as if he hates it.* "Easy money," he said aloud.

"You can't imagine how much. If you think this place is O.K., you should see Hyde's Amagansett cottage. And the horse farm in Connecticut."

"So what I wrote was true," Bech said to himself.

"If anything, you understated," Leonard assured him, his very ears now involved in the spreading folds of happiness, so that his large furry lobes dimpled.

"How sad," said Bech. "What's the point of fiction?"

"It hastens the Revolution," Leonard proclaimed, and in farewell, with hoisted palm: "Next year in Jerusalem!"

Bech needed another drink. The piano and harp were doing "Frosty the Snowman," and then the harp alone took on "Smoke Gets in Your Eyes." The room was filling up with whiteness like a steam bath. At the edge of the mob around the bar, a six-foot girl in a frilly Dior nightie gave Bech her empty glass and asked him to bring her back a Chablis spritzer. He did as he was told and when he returned to stand beside her saw that she had on a chocolate-brown leotard beneath the nightie. Her hair was an unreal red, and heavy, falling to her shoulders in a waxen Ginger Rogers roll; her bangs were cut even with her straight black eyebrows. She was heavy all over, Bech noticed, but comely, with a marmoreal humorless gaze. "Whose wife are you?" Bech asked her.

"That's a chauvinistic approach."

"Just trying to be polite."

"Nobody's. Whose husband are you?"

"Nobody's. In a way."

"Yeah? Tell me the way."

"I'm still married, but we're split up."

"What split you up?"

"I don't know. I think I was bad for her ego. Women now I guess need to do something on their own. As you implied before."

"Yeah." Her pronunciation was dead level, hovering between agreement and a grunt.

"What do *you* do, then?"

"Aah. I been in a couple a Hendy's shows."

Ah. She was a mud wrestler. Maurie Leonard in his enthusiasm for the Revolution sometimes got a few specifics wrong. The mud wrestlers *were* hookers. The give-away-nothing eyes, the calm heft held erect as a soldier's body beneath the frills. "You win or lose?" Bech asked her. He had the idea that wrestlers always proceeded by script.

"We don't look at it that way, win or lose. It's more like a dance. We have a big laugh at the end, and usually dunk the referee."

"I've always wondered, what happens if you get mud in your eyes?"

"You blink. You the writer?"

"One of the many."

"I saw you on Cavett. Nice. Smooth, but, you know, not too. You gonna stick around here long?"

"I was wondering," he said.

The girl turned her face slightly toward him—a thrilling sight, like the soft sweep of a lighthouse beam or the gentle nudging motion of a backhoe, so much smooth youth and health bunched at the base of her throat, where her nightie's lace hem clouded the issue. He felt her heavy gaze rest on the top of his head. "Maybe we could go out get a snack together afterward," she suggested. "After we circulate. I'm here to circulate."

"I am too, I guess," Bech said, his body locked numbingly around its new secret, a kind of cancer, a rampant multiplication. Men and women: what a grapple. New terms, same old pact. "Name's Lorna," his mud wrestler told him, and moved off, her leotard suspended like a muscular vase within the chiffon of her costume. He remembered Bea's soft nighties and the bottom dropped out of his excitement, leaving an acid taste. Better make the next drink weak, it looked like a long night.

"Shine On, Harvest Moon" had become the tune, and then one he hadn't heard since the days of Frankie Carle, "The Glow Worm." *Glimmer, glimmer.* The music enwrapped as with furling coils of tinsel ribbon the increasingly crowded room, or rooms; the party was expanding in the vast duplex to a boundary whereat one could glimpse those rooms stacked with the polychrome furniture that had been temporarily removed, rooms hung with paintings of rainbows and flayed nudes, bursts of color like those furious quasars hung at the outer limits of our telescopes. In the mass of churning whiteness the mud wrestlers stood firm, big sturdy girls wearing silver wigs and rabbit-fur vests and shimmery running shorts over those white tights nurses wear, or else white gowns like so many sleepwalking Lady Macbeths, or the sterilized pajamas and boxy caps of laboratory workers dealing with bacteria or miniaturized transistors; in the pallid seethe they stood out like caryatids.

Bech had to fight to get his bourbon. The piano and the harp were jostled in the middle of "Stardust" and went indignantly silent. Like a fuzzy sock being ejected by the tumble-dryer there was flung toward Bech the shapeless face of Vernon Klegg, the American Kafka, whose austere minimalist renderings of kitchen spats and dishevelled mobile homes were the rage of writers' conferences and federal and state arts councils. There was at the heart of Klegg's work a haunting enigma. Why were these heroines shrieking? Why were these heroes going bankrupt, their businesses sliding from neglect so resistlessly into ruin? Why were these children so rude, so angry and estranged? The enigma gave Klegg's portrayal of the human situation a hollowness hailed as quintessentially American; he was published with great faithfulness in the Soviet Union, as yet another illustrator of the West's sure doom, and was a pet of the Left intelligentsia everywhere. Yet one did not have to be a very close friend of Klegg's to know that the riddling texture of his work sprang from a humble personal cause: except for that dawn hour of each day when, pained by hangover and recommencing thirst, Klegg composed with sharpened pencil and yellow-paper pad his few hundred beautifully minimal words—nouns, verbs, nouns—he was drunk. He was a helpless alcoholic from whom wives, households, faculty positions, and entire neighborhoods of baffled order slid with mysterious ease. Typically in a Klegg *conte* the hero would blandly discover himself to have in his hands a butcher knife, or the broken top fronds of a rubber plant, or the buttocks of a pubescent baby-sitter. Alcohol was rarely described in Klegg's world, and he may himself not have recognized it as the element that kept that world in perpetual centrifugal motion. He had a bloated face enlarged by a white bristle that in a circle on his chin was still dark, like a panda marking. In this environment he seemed not unsober. "Hear you turned down Dakota Sioux Tech," he told Bech.

"My wife advised me to."

"Didn't know you still had a wife."

"My God, Vern, I don't. I plumb forgot."

"It happens. My fourth decamped the other day, God knows why. She just went kind of crazy."

"Same with me," Bech said. "This modern age, it puts a lot of stress on women. Too many decisions."

"Lord love 'em," Klegg said. "Who are all these cunts standing around like cops?"

"Mud wrestlers. The newest thing. Wonderful women. They keep discipline."

"About time somebody did," Klegg said. "I've lost the bar."

"Follow the crowds," Bech told him, and himself rotated away from the other writer, to a realm where the bodies thinned, and he could breathe the intergalactic dust. A stately creature swaddled in terrycloth attracted him; her face was not merely white, it was painted white, so that her eyes with their lashes stared from within a kind of mask. She smiled in welcome, and her red inner lips and gums seemed to declare an inner face of blood.

"Hey man."

"Hey," he answered.

"What juice *you* groovin' on?"

"Noble dispassion," he answered.

Her hands, Bech saw, were black, with lilac nails and palms. She was black, he realized. She was truth. The charm of liquor is not that it distorts perceptions. It does not. It merely lifts them free from their customary matrix of anxiety. America at heart is black, he saw. Snuggling into the jazz that sings to our bones, we feel that the Negro lives deprived and naked among us as the embodiment of truth, and that when the castle of credit cards collapses a black god will redeem us. The writer would have spoken more to this smiling apparition with the throat of black silk beneath her mask of rice, but Lorna, his first mud wrestler, sidled up to him and said, "You're not circulating." Her hair was as evenly, incandescently red as the glowing coil of the hot plate he cooked his lonely breakfasts on.

"Is it time to go?" he asked, like a child.

"Give it another half-hour. This is just fun for you, but Hendy makes us girls toe the line. If I skip off early it could affect my ratings."

"We don't want that."

"No we don't, ol' buddy." Before she went off again her body purposely and with only peripheral menace brushed Bech's; in the lightness of the contact her breast felt as hard as her hip. A word from Bech's deep past rose and occurred to him. *Kurveh.* The stranger who comes close.

The piano and harp were interrupted again, this time in the middle of "Stars Fell on Alabama." Henderson Hyde was up on the piano bench, making a speech about Angus Desmouches's extraordinary book. ". . . horizons. . . . not since Atget and Steichen . . . rolling back the limits of the photographic universe . . ." The albino fish in the vertical tank flurried and goggled, alarmed by the new vibrations. They were always in profile. On edge they looked like knives, like Bea's clothes in the closet. *Why is a fish like a writer?* Bech asked himself. *Because both exist in only two dimensions.* Since seeing through the black woman's white paint and obtaining for himself a fourth bourbon (neat: the party was running out of water), Bech felt the gift of clairvoyance growing within him. Surfaces parted; he had achieved X-ray vision. The white of this party was a hospital johnny beneath which lungs harbored dark patches and mud-packed arteries sluggishly pulsed. Now Angus Desmouches was up on the piano bench, saying he owed everything to his mother's sacrifices and to the nimbleness and sensitivity of his studio assistants too numerous to name. Not to mention the truly wonderful crew at Colortron Photographics. A limited number of signed copies of *White on White* could be purchased in the foyer, at the pre-Christmas price. Thank you. You're great people. Really great. The albino crowd flared and fluttered, looking for its next crumb. In the mass of white, heads and shoulders floated like photos on the back flaps of dust jackets. Bech recognized two authors, both younger than he, more prolix and polished, and saw right through them. Elegantly slim, diamond-laden Lucy Ebright, she of dazzling intellectual constructs and uncanny six-hundred-page forays into the remoter realms of history: in her work a momentous fluency passed veils of illusion before the reader's eyes everywhere but when, more and more rarely, her own threadbare Altoona girlhood was evoked. Then as it were a real cinder appeared at the heart of a great unburning fire of invention. For the one thing this beautiful conjurer of the world's riches truly understood was poverty; the humiliation of having to wear second-hand clothes, the inglorious pain of neglected teeth, the shame of watching one's grotesque parents grovel before the possessors of jobs and money—wherever such images arose, even in a psychoallegorical thriller set in the court of Kublai Khan, a jarring authenticity gave fluency pause, and the reader uncomfortably gazed upon raw truth: *I was poor*. Lucy was chatting, the sway of her long neck ever more aristocratic as her dreams succeeded in print, with the brilliant and engaging Seth Zimmer-

man, whose urbane comedies of sexual entanglement and
moral confusion revealed to Bech's paternal clairvoyance
a bitter, narrow, insistent message. *I hate you all*, Seth's
comedies said, *for forsaking Jesus.* A Puritan nostalgia, an
unreasonable longing for the barbaric promise of eternal
light beyond the slate-marked grave, a fury at all unfaith
including his own gave Zimmerman's well-carpentered
plots their uncentered intensity and his playful candor its
hostile cool. Both rising writers came up to Bech and in
all sincerity said how much they had adored *Think Big*.

"I just wished it was even longer," Lucy said in her
lazy, nasal voice.

"I wished it was even dirtier," Seth said, snorting in
self-appreciation.

"Aw, shucks," said Bech. Loving his colleagues for
their alabaster attire and for having like him climbed by
sheer desperate wits and acquired typing skill up out of
the dreary quotidian into this apartment on high, he nevertheless kept dodging glances between their shoulders to
see if his new friend in her nightie and wig were ap-
proaching to carry him off. The piano and harp, running
out of white, had turned to "Red Sails in the Sunset" and
then "Blue Skies." Radiant America; where else but here?
Still, Bech, sifting the gathering with his inspired gaze,
was not quite satisfied. Another word occurred to him.
Treyf, he thought. Unclean.

A Note About the Author

*JOHN UPDIKE was born in 1932, in Shilling-
ton, Pennsylvania, and attended Harvard College and
the Ruskin School of Drawing and Fine Arts in
Oxford, England. From 1955 to 1957 he was a staff
member of* The New Yorker, *to which he has contributed stories, poems, and book reviews. Since 1957
he has lived in Massachusetts, and is the father of
four children. The most recent of his twenty-five
previous books, the novel* Rabbit Is Rich, *won the
1982 Pulitzer Prize for Fiction, the American Book
Award for Fiction, and the National Book Critics
Circle Award.*

A Note on the Type

The text of this book was set on the Linotype in Janson, a recutting made direct from type cast from matrices long thought to have been made by the Dutchman Anton Janson, who was a practicing type founder in Leipzig during the years 1668–87. However, it has been conclusively demonstrated that these types are actually the work of Nicholas Kis (1650–1702), a Hungarian, who most probably learned his trade from the master Dutch founder Dirk Voskens. The type is an excellent example of the influential and sturdy Dutch types that prevailed in England up to the time William Caslon (1692–1766) developed his own incomparable designs from these Dutch faces.

Composed by the Maryland Linotype Composition Co., Baltimore, Maryland.

Printed and bound by the Haddon Craftsmen, Inc., Scranton, Pennsylvania.